She had come back to him, now all he had to do was find a way to keep her…

"I will take care of you, love. You will not want to leave again."

Ephraim stood, removed the sheet and, with a concentration he hadn't experienced in a while, took a hold of the body under the arms and lifted the upper half onto the table. Cradling the legs, he placed them on the cold surface. This had to be done right. There would be no second opportunity.

Bright lights revealed Angelina's condition that had been hidden by the dark bedroom: blue fingers and toes, a tinge of green throughout the waxy ashen body, opaque eyes, and mouth partially open from a swollen tongue. Ephraim didn't see or smell these states or the leaking odor of putrefaction as he admired his prized beauty.

In the remote village of Hamburg in Northern New Jersey, over the course of a few days, four young people are missing. The townspeople whisper about a "Pied Piper of Hamburg" leading children away—an appropriate analogy since the country village includes a decaying gingerbread castle within a barren fairy tale park. The police, held back by limited resources, struggle to find answers, unaware of an ugly dwarf living in seclusion in a cedar swamp miles from town. Goths, Wicca, and unknowing perversity combine to shake the sheltered hamlet to its core as Goth teenagers, Ash and Luna, befriend the undersized recluse in an effort to escape their own loneliness. But what the two teenagers finally discover will not produce a fairy tale ending.

KUDOS for *Apart*

"*Apart* is an apt title for this story. Delving into the isolation that is felt by those who fall outside of societal norms, it leads you down a twisted path wrought with murder, occultism, and misanthropy. The small town setting stirs up feelings of adolescent nostalgia, but the story quickly takes a turn into ghoulish territory and macabre madness. Milos masterfully writes characters who inspire both empathy and dread, leaving the reader aghast, but unable to resist the temptation of turning to the next page. The pace quickens with every chapter as the author drapes us in the deliciously dark world of the outcast and deranged. Both disturbing and delightful, at once, *Apart* keeps the reader hooked, forcing us to bear bizarre witness to a mind come undone." ~ Ross Acevedo, Managing Editor, *The Excelsior ReView*

"Milos tells a chilling tale of how loneliness can affect the mind and drive people to do the unthinkable. This one's a page-turner to say the least." Taylor Jones, Reviewer

"*Apart* is the story of not fitting in, the terrible loneliness that can cause, and the effect that kind of despair can have on the human psyche. It's a chilling, but poignant tale of people who live outside the norm, and the consequences such suffering can bring." ~ Regan Murphy, Reviewer

ACKNOWLEDGEMENTS

I extend my sincere thanks to Jay Milos and Patrick Ackerman for being loyal readers and to Dr. Brooke Davey, not only for her continued reading of my novels, but for her advice as well.

A story is only as good as its readers.

APART

R. James Milos

A Black Opal Books Publication

GENRE: THRILLER/MYSTERY-DETECTIVE/YOUNG ADULT

This is a work of fiction. Names, places, characters and incidents are either the product of the author's imagination or are used fictitiously, and any resemblance to any actual persons, living or dead, businesses, organizations, events or locales is entirely coincidental. All trademarks, service marks, registered trademarks, and registered service marks are the property of their respective owners and are used herein for identification purposes only. The publisher does not have any control over or assume any responsibility for author or third-party websites or their contents.

DEDICATION

To my mother, who instilled perseverance within me.

We don't always choose to recognize the lonely. They exist as ghosts outside our vision and thoughts. We are happy in this ignorance, unaware that seclusion affects some more than others and can result in deliberate or unintentional actions that force our attention.

CHAPTER 1

The father was an internist at Saint Clare's Health Center at Sussex and a drunk. He insisted on birthing his son unaccompanied at home to protect his wife's dignity as well as the expected outcome. In preparation, the doctor braced himself with cognac, several times. This affected his judgment and manipulation of steel forceps. A male baby was delivered with a skull fracture that led to an intracranial hemorrhage. The baby went into a seizure, which would cause minimal brain development problems in his formative years. The infant had inherited carpenter syndrome: a tower-shaped skull and fused index and middle finger on the right hand. This explained later why he never saw photographs of himself or most of his father's relatives. The baby also sustained facial nerve damage and a scarred face. After giving the newborn doses of phenobarbital, the father retired to his office to be consoled by the rest of the cognac bottle. During this prolonged absence, genital tract tears and injuries to the mother's uterus caused her to hemorrhage. The baby remained quiet in her arms as he listened to her blood drain and heart fade. He began life alone.

A fifty-year-old wet nurse was retained and paid handsomely to deal with his kind. The father pretended his son wasn't alive, which was better than blaming the baby for his wife's death. This, the son did himself.

A black iron fence surrounded the family cemetery in the backyard and was expanded to accommodate the mother and those of the family who would follow.

All this was told to the son later by his aged uncle who came to the old gray manor to replace the mother.

The northern corner of the attic was converted to a nursery with thick bars in a solitary small window. Later the son often wondered if this was to keep him in more than keeping anyone out. The room was decorated in midnight blue. The sun never shown in the room and, here in the dark, he was allowed to hide. In summer, he suffocated in the heat and was only allowed out at night. In winter, a small pot belly stove installed in the middle of the garret provided minimal warm. He was fascinated with the bright dancing flames and then the attractiveness of glowing embers. This was a dimension he could escape into and live a different life. He found a metal curtain rod and continually poked at the fire and cinders. This was something he had control over.

The best and strongest tutors from outside the county were hired so he wouldn't have to bear the indignity of schooling with others. They signed a contract not to reveal their experiences. All the tutors, though, quickly disengaged their services because of his appearance and seemingly inability to learn.

His friends were the spiders in the corners and his uncle. He didn't realize his true condition, however, since he wasn't aware of any other existence.

Because of the syndrome, the boy became obese, but strong. He would never reach beyond a four-foot-eleven-inch stature.

Near his thirteenth birthday, a night-time fire originated in the nursery and destroyed part of the house and the father with it. The boy disappeared in an oak grove, nursing burnt fingers. He watched with fascination as the blaze consumed his world. Firefighters with yellow helmets ran around spraying water on charred and burning wood. The destruction warmed him in a way the father never had.

His uncle severed the endless cycle of tutors and started to rebuild the house, maintaining the Edwardian style in keeping with family traditions: steep slate pitched roof, dormers, gables, a large wrap around front porch, and balconies edged with timber railings and fretwork patterns. The boy was given a true bedroom and the admonishment to never go out in the day, except at dusk to split wood for the kitchen fire.

The tall gray painted-brick structure rose above the swamp and fit well into the stark landscape of the estate. It was stronger than ever. The workmen both frightened and attracted him with their actions and loud purposes. He stayed hidden, listening to the noise and cursing. Once, when the last truck of the day had disappeared, he ventured out and smelled sweat, old cigarette butts, and sawdust. Near a crumbled beer can, he found a magazine. It had photographs of naked women. He stared at the smooth skin and forced smiles. They were foreign, beautiful, and so out of his reach. The boy was fascinated. This was a world beyond the house and grounds. He brought the magazine to Uncle to ask him so many questions. Uncle snatched away the "filth." His bald head turned red and his nose, except for a large wart, showed thin red lines as he squeezed the magazine and shook his fist.

He crumbled the pages and tried to speak. "This! This!" was all he could manage as spit and drool issued from his nearly toothless mouth. The boy fled to the cellar where he remained—feeding on preserved fruit and vegetables and toileting in the corner by the coal bin—for the rest of the week till the workmen were finished.

Uncle told him what the father did not but what the boy had come to know. Some of the family was different. They were special, not meant for outside society. The family did not need anyone. They were apart, above all sinful needs. The boy accepted this judgment without fully realizing what Uncle meant.

Uncle and the boy stayed inside the dark dwelling, linked to the world through a small gray telephone line. The house had become a fortress in the middle of twenty fallow acres bordered by a state park. Black wrought iron spiked gates protected the driveway entrance and opened electronically to admit only service vans and grocery delivery. Uncle and the boy were content in their isolation, but then the boy knew no better.

When the boy was seventeen, Uncle died. He simply slumped over while eating brisket. The boy wrapped him in a table cloth and dragged the lifeless bundle to the cemetery. He placed him in the cemetery's soft earth near the weeping willow. No marker. Nothing to tell of Uncle's absence. No words to mark his passing. The boy did watch over the grave to see if flowers would bloom, indicating Uncle had led a good life, or if only weeds prospered, indicating evil. Neither happened. Unkempt grass flourished.

As family custom dictated, the boy drew all curtains closed and stopped all clocks for a week. He didn't bother to wind the clock after the week since he did not know the correct time.

The boy continued his existence, using the black Bakelite telephone and the accounts established by Uncle. He had taught the boy these elementary functions for this time of his life. The boy left checks on the porch under a rock and hid till delivery vans vanished. A safe, hidden in the cellar, contained large amounts of cash for such time as needed. The marsh was his garbage dump. It attracted the only companions he had: deer, raccoons, birds, rats, and sometimes black bear that, despite their mass and strength, would run at the sight of him.

As he grew, he wore the father's or Uncle's clothes. The lawn also grew uncut and unkempt and, with each year, oak leaves carpeted the driveway disturbed only by the periodic deliveries. With each new seasonal layer, the boy became more aware of the edges of loneliness.

He was now twenty and stood in what remained of the former nursery. Faint burnt smells, even now, permeated the area. Moonlight tried to enter but was defeated a few feet from the window. He stared toward the dark woods through the bars, still wondering about the meaning of the irons and why they had been left there. He had been changing. Something was happening. The young man had uneasy feelings he could not explain. Inside his body, emptiness stirred and rattled in search of...of what he did not know. He did know that he was not far from the boundary of despair and deep into longing. He hadn't had a conversation with another human in over three years.

The young man could not even remember his parents now. He missed Uncle. He created memories, but they were all depressing. He had a need he could not explain and no one to talk with. The young man searched Uncle's belongings looking for something, but he did not know what it was.

In the north woods near the house, there was a deep ancient swamp. The water was black and rotten. Thin pyramidal cedars fed on the misery of their surroundings. He walked there often at twilight, finding comfort in the dead trees and damp ground. Snakes swam away and frogs hid when he approached but, if he was still, they returned and he could enjoy their company. Lately though, the young man had stayed away. He became aware of his reflection in the stagnant pools. He studied himself. He knew he was ugly and seeing only himself, just him and the emptiness of the sky above, created an ache, a hollowness in his being that caused him to run and run, filling his lungs with fetid air, exhausting his body till he dropped into the sour softness of the swamp.

He did belong here, though. This he knew above all else. He fed on the swamp's misery, delighted in its desolation. It too was lonely. They had only each other.

Not long ago, he began to move through the swamp at night when he could not see his likeness. Dusky smells embraced him. The wet ground pulled at his feet—the sucking sound was pleasing.

He hesitated at times and slowly, slowly sank deep into the miry warm embrace of the slime. He lifted a boot and let it slide in again. Though the ground was rank and decayed, he was not afraid of miasma. Around him, the swamp groaned with life. It was a pleasurable sensation.

Sometimes, he entered the marsh barefooted. Deep inside it, the ooze slid between his toes and licked at his legs. The muck was silky and forgiving. He would stagger till he was spent. The young man could not stay away. This was his family now.

It was a cold September. He huddled inside his wool blanket. Yesterday's porridge bowl remained on a white porcelain enamel kitchen table in front of him. He felt a fever, perhaps with it the dizzy freedom of sickness. Recently, he went naked and rolled in the supple still-warm water, smearing mud over his body. He began to touch himself. The excitement brought his thoughts back to the magazine he had found. He liked the stimulation, but the result frightened him.

It was gloaming. He sat in the kitchen and stared out a window at the woods. Jackdaws called on barren branches. Called for what? Behind the trees, almost hidden, he spotted movement. He did not make out its form. It was not animal—it was large and red. Red and in his swamp! For a moment, he considered investigating, but only for moment. What—what if there were people there? He was curious, but cautious. Something drew him to this mystery, though.

Paralyzed with indecision, he sat and watched. Shortly into early night, two beams of light thrust forward, and the red moved again retracing its path. His fever continued and his skin burned, but still he was compelled to uncover this obscurity. He waited till the dark settled deep into the earth. Then the young man followed a calling he could not ignore.

He opened the kitchen door. A lightning bug flew in. This could only mean that someone was going to die. He hesitated, but the call was strong, and he shut the door, leaving the firefly to roam the house.

He was vaguely aware of moisture slowly running down his legs as he moved toward the trees. He hurried through the swamp. The tracks were just visible in the faint moonlight: tire ruts led from and to the highway. The ground at the edge of the wetland was firm and hard, able to support the weight of an automobile. He stood stunned, shocked. He never knew this path existed. He never knew it was so accessible.

Someone had ignored the *No Trespassing* and *Keep Out* signs along the perimeter of the estate. Someone had driven between the trees to make a road. Someone had touched his swamp. For what? He searched the ground, running his hands over and near the end of the tire tracks. Clean, intact. Apparently, no one had emerged from the car. But someone had been here—someone had violated his swamp. Why was it here? What had happened in the car?

Frustration built inside him and caused him to grunt and stamp on the tracks. His face flushed and his body heated. The young man raced back into the swamp and was calmed in its rhythms and gentle stirrings. Perhaps the red would be back. For the first time in a long while, he looked forward to something.

Six days had gone and no red. It was six nights now that he stayed inside, fearful of being seen—and fearful that, being seen, the visitor would run. He didn't know which one was more frightening. His thoughts were clouded. The fever chills held on. He would wait one more day, just one more night.

Daylight was leeching out and a cool late September evening was forming. The young man began to relax from his foolish thoughts. Fever. It was the fever. There was no red. There would be no contact. It was his place to be apart. He was different. He placed his dinner aside and prepared to leave the kitchen, but there! Behind the trees! Lights once again! He sprinted as best as he could out of the house, the blood in his head racing faster than in his heart. The fever caused him to stumble. He thrashed out blindly. His feet and legs were cut by thorns and naked shrub branches. He became quiet as he neared the far tree and saw a red car, a bright red car. He hunkered down and looked. There was no one about. He crept closer. The windows were steamed to opaque. The car rocked slowly and he heard struggling inside. People! Perhaps fighting! Closer. Without disturbing so much as a fallen twig the young man crept closer. He could only see partial shadows through the windows. Something was happening inside. Now laughter. At first, he did not recognize it. What was going on? He placed his head near the glass. There was movement inside like wriggling larvae. And new sounds. Soft moans and gasps. The young man was excited without knowing why. He wanted to enter the car. His hand reached for the door handle. The handle was smooth and hard. He grasped it and held on. It pulled and pushed his hand as the car rolled and the noises increased in volume and emotion. His heart was racing. He lifted the handle. The movement stopped.

"What was that?"

"What?"

"Someone's outside."

"What the hell you talking about? Forget it. Come on!"

"No, no. I know someone's outside. I saw something through the window."

"This place is deserted. No one comes here."

"Vince!"

"All right. All right."

The door opened and a man stepped out half naked. From his hiding place, the young man saw a woman inside the car. She was propped up on her elbows in the front seat. Short light brown hair was plastered on her forehead. Her breasts were glistening with sweat—her panties were around one ankle.

"There's no one here." Vince climbed back into the car and over the woman.

The young man watched the car begin to rock again and he heard her low song.

Long after they left, he remained. He was afraid if he moved from this spot the memories of her full breasts and pink nipples would fade. The young man trembled, but not from fever. Later, he limped through the swamp thinking of seeing her again, feeling a stimulation he had not felt since he discovered that magazine.

The next night, he hid, waiting. Mosquitoes ignored him. His blood was not sweet enough. The car did not return. He straggled back through the mud. The young man continued nightly vigils, in hope of a second showing. The following night they still did not come.

Four days later a red automobile rolled to a stop five feet from his hiding place. The windows were clear. He watched as the driver unbuttoned her blouse, slipped his hand behind her under garment and cupped a breast. The young man gasped as the driver revealed the soft white breast. He placed her nipple in his mouth and began to suck. She smiled and reclined, rubbing his head. The young man was excited, more than at any other time in his life. He needed to get closer. The man slipped her blouse off completely and unlatched that piece of clothing underneath. She worked his shirt and then his pants. As she slid down on the seat, he positioned himself on top of her. The young man watched this exotic dance in fascination as the windows began to fog.

He moved closer, listening to her muted groaning. He could not see everything he needed to know. He peered in the window and saw only shapes in rhythmic motions. His head was next to the glass when a hand wiped the moisture and the inside of the car was visible. The man glared at him. Below, she started to scream, but the young man could not leave. Her legs were spread around the man and her nipples were taut. The young man could not stop staring.

The driver swiftly pushed the door open. "God damn it!"

The young man fell and scrambled on his back into the bushes.

The driver turned in circles buckling his belt. "You freak! Where the hell are you?"

The young man was hidden but the driver moved in his direction, bellowing for effect, "Come out here, you bastard, come out!"

The driver came near the hiding place. Even in the dark, rage was visible on his face. A rock was in the young man's hand. He leapt up, swung, hit the driver in the head, and was surprised—the contact was stimulating. The driver grabbed his head and backed up, stumbled, and fell. The young man jumped on top of him and pounded the rock into the face. The driver tried to protect himself, instead of hitting the young man—he was beaten till he became motionless.

The car tried to start. The woman was screaming and trying to get away. The young man went to her, not to tell her he was sorry or to hurt her, but to feel her breasts like other did. She saw the young man and screamed even louder. He reached his bloody hands out. She retreated to the passenger side and attempted to open the locked door. Her screaming increased in pitch. He entered the automobile—she started to claw at him. He seized her throat and squeezed to stop the screaming. His grasp was slippery with blood, but the hold worked. He tried to explain that he did not mean her any harm. Her eyes were wide. She struggled to pull the hands away. He held on till she was still.

Her breasts were supple and smooth. They became slightly pink as the young man massaged them. He was trembling and grew excited. He made an effort to imitate what he had witnessed. He was clumsy at first, but became more adept each time. It was more than pleasure—it was a togetherness that he had never experienced. He took her left breast into his mouth and suckled till he fell asleep.

In the morning, the young man's limbs were cramped from spending the night in the front seat. He gazed at his lover again and felt the excitement return. He left the automobile to clean up. Animals and stray dogs had found the driver in the dark hours. He looked more like the young man now—how fitting. The young man gently lowered the woman to the ground and then placed the driver in the car. Thanks to Uncle's lessons, he slipped the shift into neutral and pushed the automobile and its cargo into the swamp. The water was not deep, though, and the car was partially visible. He placed branches around it to cover the bright red. Hopefully, it might look like a beaver den.

He held her from behind her shoulders occasionally touching her breasts as he dragged her home and up to his parents' bedroom. He gently set her on the bed. She was beautiful. She was now the only thing of value he had ever owned. The young man called her Angelina after his mother.

Every morning he dressed her in his mother's clothes and combed her hair. He was not insane—but he did not know what sanity was. He did know she was dead, but she brought him pleasure and he could not part with that.

Later, he erased the heel marks she had made leading to the house. He checked the swamp area each day for other visitors. The automobile seemed to sink more each day. He arranged more branches on it. No others came. He uselessly hoped these two might not be missed. Venturing near the road, he did his best to hide any evidence that a car had entered the woods—all the time being careful not to be seen.

It had been nearly a week now. He was certain she enjoyed their love as much as he did. Blood bubbles had stopped forming from her nose. Angelina's stiffness had gone, but she looked ill. Her eyes had flattened and a terrible grin formed on her withered mouth. Her coloring was changing to a marbleized appearance. Although her breasts had shrunk, her stomach had swollen and he wondered if she was pregnant. She smelled like the swamp—

there was comfort in that, though. He knew she must be buried, but he could not bring himself to do it. He could not part with her yet. The young man did not want to be alone again. Angelina had brought fullness to his life. He lifted up her skirt, smiled, and felt himself grow hard. She was so much better than the magazine. Her skin had become damp and made it easier for him to love her again. Uncle was wrong! It was not filth, but beauty. He realized that soon she would leave, but not today, not today.

That was his beginning. Now this was his ending. The young man felt no regrets, except for being lonely.

CHAPTER 2

Nothing much ever happened in Hamburg Borough in the northern tip of Sussex County, New Jersey. The total crime index was nine out of a national average of one hundred. No murders, rapes, robberies, or vehicle thefts. Black bear problems, snow plows damaging mailboxes, and winter parking regulations were the big worries for the season coming up.

October was proving to be a cold month and this signified rough weather ahead.

Hamburg, once known as "The Children's Town," was on the road to oblivion. The population was dwindling each year, as industry and opportunities failed to materialize.

A once-famous attraction and a mill on Gingerbread

Castle Road off Route 23 that helped grow the area were closed and forgotten.

The Munsee Delawares were the first to occupy land located near the Gingerbread Castle. Immigrants came and wounded the earth, looking for minerals—and, as a by-product of this greed, the natives were killed or chased from their home. In 1768, trees were felled, ground became entombed, as Joseph Sharp built ironworks on the Wallkill River. The Wheatsworth Grain Mill was built over the abandoned works in 1808 and the buildings sold many times since. The warehouse and multiple-storied offices now remained empty of commerce but full of decay: graffiti, old couches, building material, burnt rooms, blackened doorways, and charred floorboards. Shattered windows and collapsed roofs let memories escape and wandering souls enter. A plywood sign lettered in red was stuck on a mound of rubble—*Licensed by State of New Jersey for Asbestos Work License No. 00723*. The five-acre facility, once a major employer of Hamburg, had become a tax burden and major eyesore for the deteriorating borough. Teenagers had begun to occupy first-floor offices, smoking marijuana and socializing, since Hamburg didn't have its own shopping mall. This ended shortly when tetrahydrocannabinol or reality scared all but the brave away from ghostly shadows, desolate surroundings, and dirty walls that echoed sounds not recognizable. The structures stood vacant, except for occasional visits of the curious and desperate lovers and the traces of their passages: used condoms, old damp mattresses, melted candles, forgotten flashlights, and snack wrappers. Paint continued to sweat from the ceilings and halls. Mortar-softened, bricks fell, and foundations crumbled. Nature was in the slow process of taking back what once was hers. Too costly to raze, the ruins had scant hope of resurrection. Residents preferred to look away as they sped past the mammoth tomb of continued failure.

The three-story plaster-and-stone Gingerbread Castle and a three-acre park were a tri-state fairy tale venue for families. It was built in 1930 by Frederick Bennett, the owner of the adjacent lot housing Wheatsworth Mill. After Bennett had seen the Metropolitan Opera production of Hansel and Gretel, he commissioned the Viennese architect, Joseph Urban, to design the castle and grounds. The castle was decorated with cake-like stucco, elaborate window designs, terraces, and finials. The park reached its popularity in the fifties and sixties. Electronics and other technological advancements in entertainment decreased visitations. The park became too costly to maintain and was abandoned. Frequent fires, weather, and long neglect resulted in moldering ruins on an overgrown hillside. Vines tried to crack the shell of a seven-foot statue of Humpty Dumpty at the castle entrance, unaware of the hard mortar within. Witches clung to the circular towers of the castle and knights on horses had fallen, without the beliefs of children to give them strength. Jack and Jill had truly tumbled down, and chicken wire sprang from their broken bodies. Painted gnomes were disappearing forever under harsh sun and forces of unrelenting climate change. Other storybook characters were peeking through debris and vegetation, looking for meaning. Candy Cane Lane resembled a line of question marks as the weather bleached and birds stained the inverted red and white meat hooks. The houses of the three little pigs, other storied structures, snack stands, and shops had collapsed upon themselves, surrendering to the harsh reality of indifference. Rails, that once carried a small-scale train full of excited children and contented adults around the grounds, rusted toward dust. The Gingerbread Castle Park was now a mausoleum for childhood innocence.

These two rejected sites were monuments to the bleak future of this forgotten rural town. New Jersey Routes 23 and 94 intersected in the borough and seemed to lead away from the town rather than to it.

Sergeant Jay Hurray sat among two rows of two desks crammed in a windowless, pecan-paneled room at the police department headquarters on Orchard Street. He absentmindedly rubbed the bristles on his head—hair cut so short that color wasn't discernible, cut short to mask his growing widow's peak, cut short to make him look formidable. Soon, he would be bald like his maternal grandfather. Time was moving fast—faster than his ambitions. Jay squinted at two missing person reports, promising himself again that he would go to the optometrist on Route 23 for a checkup. These reports were as exciting as borough police work got. The last "Missing" investigation was two years ago for a teenager who was found the next night at Doc's Bar in back of a dumpster, unconscious from binging.

These reports concerned Vincent Maroni and Dawn Portny who were both nineteen. He would have to interview some people and then wait till the two came home or revealed themselves elsewhere. Hurray already had filed a Missing Person Report for the National Crime Information Centers Record Entry and used the New Jersey Law Enforcement Telecommunications System to broadcast the incidents on a statewide basis. After a couple of days, he was sure, he would be able to close the file.

Jay categorized this as Voluntary Missing Adults, VMA—adults who were reported missing, but probably left of their own free will, since it seemed more likely they were runaways. There wasn't any New Jersey law for leaving home involving over-eighteen-year-olds. They were known to be a serious couple. Their parents, like so many here, had shown no interest in their school activities or ambitions after graduation. Concerned only about daily existence, they were probably unaware of their children's absence, even though they lived at home. Friends of the two had filed separate reports.

Paper pushing and boring interviews—not the exciting law enforcement life Jay had envisioned. This certainly was not the expectations he had when he entered Seton Hall University for a degree in criminal justice.

That seemed so long ago. However, married with two children, a house, and, of course, a dog, he found it wasn't a bad position to be in—it was the only position now. His time here offered slow suffocation rather than breathtaking promises.

In any event, this work was better than patrolling to make sure the four crossing guards were on duty during school bus runs.

Missing persons took priority over property-related crimes, and the only other active concern was graffiti on the Highlands Connect Bus Station. Jay rifled through his files to find the Missing Person File, Data Collection Entry Guide. After briefly perusing it, he planned to drive to the parents' residences to obtain photos, DNA from both sets of parents, and personal objects that might contain Vincent and Dawn's DNA. Then on to interview Randy Mcgreen and Janette Sohouser, the friends who filed the reports.

Jay left the brick, single-story headquarters under overcast autumn skies, entered the ten-year-old unlocked Ford police car, and headed north on 94 past the Rite Aid, Sonny's Bar & Grill, and the Healthy Place food store then on Lawrence Street to the Maroni's light blue cottage. Tony Maroni was a driver in Lafayette for a food-service industry. His wife, Maria, was a waitress at Sonny's.

The sergeant was about to leave after waiting a decent interval, cursing silently that he would have to return using his family time for professional business, when Maria finally answered his knocks. She was dressed in a lime green terry cloth bathrobe smoking a cigarillo. All she needed were large curlers in her short graying hair to be a complete caricature.

"Yes?"

"Mrs. Maroni, may I speak with you for a moment?"

"Oh Christ! What's Tony done now? Did he get into another fight? Did he miss work again?"

"No, it's not about Tony."

"What then?"

"When's the last time you saw Vincent?"

"Vince?" She took a puff, thinking, coughed, "I guess it was…ah…I don't know, maybe yesterday?"

"Mrs. Maroni, a missing person report has been filed for your son. May I come in?"

"What? Sure." She backed up and moved to a lumpy sofa covered with a floral bed sheet. "This about Vince, not Tony? Vince is missing?"

Jay gave her a minute to process the information. "Yes, ma'am. Apparently he has been for almost three days now."

"Really?"

"Yes."

"I guess I hadn't noticed. He comes and goes, ya know."

"Do you know a Dawn Portny"?

"That slut. Well, that explains it. He probably ran off

with her. She was always loose, you know what I mean? Always showing her tits with low cut blouses and wearing short dresses to flaunt her stuff."

"You didn't know he was gone?"

"Why should I? He's not a kid anymore. He's got a job at Harper's Garage. I don't check on him every day. I have a job and ain't always home all the time. I've got my own problems, ya know, like my worthless husband, the bastard! Sometimes Vince stays at his friend's house or at the garage when he's working on something special. Jesus Christ, it's only been, what, three days. What's the fuss?"

"Well, I'm sure he's okay, but since a report was filed, I need to go through procedures."

Maria took another drag, shrugged her shoulders. "Fine, fine, let's get it over with. I need to get ready for work."

Jay reviewed his check list. "What is Vince's full name?"

"Vincent John Maroni."

"Date of birth?"

Maria seemed to think for moment before she answered, "September 6, 1995."

"Social security number?"

"I don't know that!"

"That's okay. What dentist do you go to?"

"We don't have coverage for dental."

"Please describe Vince."

"Um, maybe five eleven, long brown hair. Kinda muscular, ya know what I mean?"

"Any distinguishing marks?

"Scars on his legs and arms from rough housing as a boy and work at the garage. No tats that I know of."

"Who did he hang out with?"

"Besides the whore? Maybe the guys at the garage or his friends."

"Do you know their names?"

"Well, Bill Harper and…" Maria rolled her eyes and pursed her lips as if this was a difficult question, "Randy, Randy Mcgreen."

"Anyone else?"

"No, not that I know off hand—some high school friends maybe."

"Does Vincent own a vehicle?"

"Yes."

Jay was becoming frustrated with the lack of information he was receiving. "What make and color?"

"Ah, red. I don't know what make."

"I don't suppose you know the license plate number?"

"No."

"Do you have a recent photo of Vincent?"

"I'll have to look."

"I'll need to swab the inside of your mouth."

"What for?"

"DNA."

"What good is that?"

"In case we find a body that is not readily identifiable."

"What? You think Vince is dead?"

"No, not at all—it's all procedural. I'll also need something personal of Vince's. Maybe a comb with hair follicles, a toothbrush—" He doubted there would be a toothbrush.

"Listen, I have to get to work, or they'll dock me."

"I'm sure it won't take a minute." Jay took a sterilized swab and vial from the kit he brought. "Please open."

Maria gave him an annoyed look. The swab was rubbed against the inside of her cheek and placed in the vial.

"Photograph and comb?"

Disappearing into other parts of the house, she returned with a framed picture and a black comb. The photo must have been taken years ago: a young Vincent posed with a bat in Little League uniform.

"Anything more recent?"

"Listen, I really don't have the time. Check with the high school for his yearbook photo. He's all right. You said so yourself. He can look after himself, anyways. He's probably holed up somewhere, fucking his brains out with that piece of trailer trash."

"I'll return these items."

"Whatever."

Jay departed, hoping he'd meet with better results at the Portny's residence.

The yellow vinyl double-width mobile home was on Jennings Road. As Jay pulled into the driveway, Carl Portny was exiting the house.

"Can I help you, Officer?"

"I'd like to have a minute of your time."

"I'm leaving for work. I have the late shift."

"This is important. It's about your daughter, Dawn."

"Crap. What's she up to now?"

"She's missing."

"Missing what?"

"She hasn't been seen for over three days."

"Did you check with her friend Janette?"

"Janette Sohouser was the one who reported her missing."

"Oh. She usually hangs out at Janette's house. She's independent. I'm not worried. What could happen around here?"

"Do you know Vincent Marconi?"

"Yeah, I know that wop. Unfortunately, he and Dawn are pretty tight. She doesn't have the brains of a worm and he has the ambition of rock. The perfect couple."

"I need to ask you some more questions, Mr. Portny."

"Look, I travel to Newton for my job."

"What do you do?"

"I'm a machinist. And what does that have to do with anything?

"Does Dawn own a car?"

"We can't afford that. Maybe if the Mill was still open and I had a better job."

"When was the last time you saw her?"

"I don't know. I work nights and sleep days. Ask her mother."

"I intend to. Is she home?"

"Yes."

"Okay, I need you to go back inside so I can take some DNA samples and ask a few more questions."

"This is ridiculous. She's almost a grown woman. She knows how to handle herself. Wait, samples of what?"

"The cells inside your mouth. I'll explain. Perhaps, can we go in?" Jay moved closer to Portny in an intimidating gesture, blocking his path to the driveway.

"Fine, fine. But let's make this quick, okay?"

Inside, Carl addressed an empty room, "Alice, a cop is here asking about Dawn."

Alice rushed out of the kitchen, wiping her hands with a dish towel. "What happened? Is she hurt?"

"We don't know, ma'am. I need to ask both of you some questions."

Alice grabbed her husband's arm and pulled him down on a tan couch. Her face started to take on fear.

"Do you know of any reason Dawn might have to run away?"

"On, my gosh, no. She has Vince and her position at the beauty parlor. You know, she's quite attractive and has a real flair with hair design. Everyone says so."

"Vince is missing as well."

Mrs. Portny's face lost more color. "Him, too?"

"Yes." Jay consulted his notes and asked the same questions as he had with the Marconis and basically discovered the same lack of knowledge with only a little more interest.

A recent photograph and hair brush were delivered and bagged.

The next stop was Harper's Garage on Route 94. The small two-bay white building stood one hundred yards off the road. Used cars for sale parked along the drive made the garage seem more active than it really was.

Bill Harper owned the repair shop and serviced all the police vehicles. Jay was familiar with Bill because of this and the fact that Harper's was the only place in town to call for towing damaged and illegally parked cars.

"Bill!" Jay called to the backside of a squat figure straining over the front grill of an '88 Oldsmobile.

"Yeah?" Bill answered over his shoulder, yanking on a torque wrench.

"I need to ask you some questions."

"I'm a little busy now. If you come back—" Bill faced his questioner. "Oh, Sergeant. Sure. What can I do for you?" Harper was always deferential to the police, his biggest client.

"Vincent Marconi. Do you know him?"

"Sure do. He was a good mechanic."

"Was?"

"Well, he hasn't been around for days. I assumed he quit."

"Would you happen to know where he is?"

"No, sir, I don't. Maybe you should ask Randy Mcgreen."

"Did Vincent appear to be upset the last time you saw him?"

"No, not that I noticed."

"Okay, thanks."

"Wait, don't you want to speak to Randy? He's inside." Harper indicted the right bay.

Randy finished a long drag on his joint before he saw the sergeant enter through the side door. He threw the joint behind him and reflexively waved his hands trying to aerate the blue cloud around him.

"Never mind that. Are you Randy Mcgreen?"

"Yes, sir," Randy coughed out.

"You filed a missing person report for Vincent Marconi?"

"Yes, sir."

"Why?

"Why?"

"Yes, why do you think he is missing?"

"Vince and me are tight, you know? Like he would never do anything serious without telling me, man."

"Are you sure of that?"

"Damn straight. We're best buddies."

"Do you have any guesses where he would be now?"

"Don't know, but I'll bet my ass he's with Dawn."

"Dawn Portny?"

"Yeah."

"When's the last time you saw him?"

"Uh, right before his date with Dawn."

"When was that?"

"Saturday night. I haven't seen him since, and it's not like him to just disappear like that."

"Did he say where he was going with Dawn?"

"Naw, nothing."

"Was anyone mad at him?"

"Mad? No. A lot of the guys are jealous since he's boning Dawn, but mad? He's full of himself, but, ya know, Vince is likable."

"Okay. If you see him, please contact the police department so we can end our investigation. People are worried about him. He's not in any trouble with us. Understand?"

"Yes, sir, will do."

Jay found Janette Sohouser waiting tables at Granny's Pancake House & Grill on Route 23.

After asking the same questions and receiving the same answers, the sergeant ended hours of interviewing with hardly any new information. These kids had better show up fast.

CHAPTER 3

Night had choked the day and muted the street lamps. Countryside silence blanketed the houses. Brown, brittle autumn leaves lay listless where they had fallen. Yellow light diffused through square windows indicated life within. It did not travel far outside—the dark ate it with a hunger. Some portals were obscure. An ambiguity of time settled over Hamburg as the night deepened. Most of its people were content to just exist and ride the darkness out.

Ash sat on the floor, absently fingering one of the Celtic crosses around his neck, waiting for inspiration for the next diary entry. Emo music boomed through speakers in the background. His bedroom was dark, a comforting darkness to hide in. Black plastic bags had been taped on the two windows. Six electric candles provided the only light source. His parents wouldn't allow flames or permit him to paint the walls deep purple. This was his life—unsympathetic overseers at home and days of being bullied at high school.

Trepidation is only a reaction instilled in us by doctrinaires and propaganda from the uncaring. Ash edged the candle closer and carefully drew a ghoulish skull stretched in fearful agony beneath that entry then penned, *There is exquisiteness in shadows that cloud our minds.*

"Korbin, come down for dinner."

He had told his mother many times that his chosen name now was Ash, but she didn't listen. No one listened.

Ash hid his diary in the closet.

"So how did the day go, son?" his father asked as Ash slumped in dining room chair. The school psychologist had advocated for more parental interest in Ash's activities.

"Fine."

"Anything happened today?"

Ash wanted to say that Jud Robinson and his clique of other seniors had stuffed his head in the toilet and flushed it in the morning then pushed and bumped him into the hall lockers, knocked textbooks from his arms, and called him a fag because of his mascara and purple fingernail polish like they did almost every single day. Robinson's current girlfriend, Brenda, always made sour faces, teasingly shook her tits, and stuck out her tongue just to be one with the group, but he replied, "Nothing much, just the usual."

Ash's mother brushed a strand of black self dyed hair from his face. "Sweetie, I don't know how you can see."

Ash turned away from the endearment and touch.

No one understood him. Everyone was so concerned about normalcy and ignorant about the intricacies of life. Dullness and stupidity were inherent within a staid environment. The brilliant and cerebral were shunned and tormented. The only grace was the beauty of nature.

"So what music are you listening to now?"

"Have you been spying on me?"

"No, son, it's just that the music is so loud we can't help but hear."

"Dismember, Bauhaus, Sisters of Mercy, and the Banshees, not that you would appreciate them."

"You're probably correct on that, Korbin."

"I've told you my name now is Ash!" Ash used this as an excuse to leave the table and retreated to his room. Turning on his music, he sat and brooded. It was sad though noble to be apart—different, above the common.

"This isn't working, Dorothy. I don't know how to get through to him. We need to tear down that damned plastic window covering and removed the skull images, candles, and all the other crap and just apply some good old parenting like my father did."

"No, no. We need to give it time. Dr. Fairlin said it

won't be easy. We just need to show love and compassion. This is only a phase he's going through."

"I don't know. I'm getting tired of it. His attitude is getting to be impossible."

"Give it just a little more time, dear. You know he's more moody at Halloween. Perhaps after all the holidays we can all visit the doctor again."

"Okay. But I tell you, Dorothy, no good can come from this and the sooner we end it the better."

Yes, yes. Finish your dinner, Henry. I'll bring some up to Korbin—Ash, I mean."

🙰🙰🙰

After saying his goodbye and gratitude, the young man wrapped Angelina in the bed sheets she had rested on and began to haul her to the hole dug apart from the family cemetery—he did not want to share her with others. He winced each time her head bumped on stair steps, but he did the best he could. Gently, he placed her in the ground then packed the earth hard so the black bears wouldn't disturb her.

The mattress was stained from pools of liquid, but it was too large for him to do anything. He closed the door leaving everything as it was. There were other bedrooms in this large house.

The young man sat inside, staring at her grave remembering the good times. She must come back. He never knew true loneliness until he lost her. Angelina would return to him. This he hoped—this he knew.

He watched where red had been, hoping for her to show again. He checked the area every day. Branches had drifted away—only the car roof remained visible. He recovered it with a layer of black swamp ooze.

He removed the logs placed to hinder entry. Something had again awakened inside of him and he desperately needed Angelina to visit again, but he did not know how to find her. She had to find him.

෧෨෧

Ash told his parents he was going out to stay with a friend and go trick or treating the next day. They were so relieved that he had a friend, no questions about names or places were asked. Henry looked forward to a respite from the noise Ash called music.

Most of his stuff was already there. He just needed to pack a sleeping bag, bottles of water, tomato juice, snack cakes, chalk, and his diary.

The full moon was out tonight. Tomorrow would be Halloween when he could freely walk the streets and have no one whisper or point. Few knew that Halloween began 2,000 years ago with an ancient Celtic festival, when people would create bonfires, sacrifice animals, and wear costumes to ward off ghosts. On the night of every October thirty-first, the spirits of the dead returned to earth, caused trouble, and damaged crops, but they also communicated with Celtic priests, Druids, to predict the future. Pope Gregory III incorporated this celebration of Samhain within a construct he created and named All Saint's Day to replace Samhain with a Christian-oriented holiday. The evening before the celebration became known as All Hollow's Eve, which morphed into Halloween.

Now Halloween was all commercial and greed just like Christmas. The stupid masses had no idea of the lineage they were celebrating. Greed had triumphed again.

Ash stood on the front porch of the cream-colored Colonial. No one was about yet. At the end of the driveway, he turned on Oak. It was a short walk past Falcon Ridge Way, across Route 23 to his destination: the Gingerbread Castle Park.

Inside the park were the remains of the once-colorful gingerbread house, home to the fairy tale witch who tried to bake children. It was an ideal place. Part of the roof exposed the stars and the rest offered a private sanctuary.

The park was surrounded by chain-link fence with three strands of barbed wire on top. The police or current owners never patrolled the area so several links had been cut for entry. Ash moved swiftly up a hill to the northeast corner, found his opening, and walked past the disused enchanted playground. Rusting poles stretched to the sky from the ground, as if they were bones of a mythical beast trying to resurrect itself. He turned right on Mother

Goose Lane. The full moon illuminated the area in a silver veil so navigation was certain. Ash felt the draw as he neared the sad structure.

Bushes and trees grew around the decomposing cottage. Glass had been smashed, using loose bricks from the building. Graffiti tried to mask the whimsical with lewd remarks. Breaching man and nature's guard, Ash slid a board from a broken window, rearranged vines, and entered his truly private place. A smell of oldness, a smell of ancients, always greeted him in this refuge.

Ash lit candles on shelves that cast flowing shadows across the decaying room. The walls were weeping strips of paint. No laughter remained within the dead fibers of the wood. No joy had been embedded in the mute plaster. The walls were now void and lifeless—they offered no record of what once was. Weeds tried to flourish between the floor boards, but lack of sun and nutrients withered them to brown spindly stalks.

Ash emptied his backpack, retrieved his Wiccan wooden-handled knife—bought at Sears and now called an athame—and other objects from hidden places. He positioned bowls of water and ordinary salt on a cinder block altar in the middle of the room and zipped up his leather jacket against the chill.

Ash practiced his own form of Wicca, practiced it alone. Not trained in British Traditional Wicca, Ash learned and interpreted rituals from the Internet. He didn't belong to a coven or circle. There simply wasn't interest in sparsely populated Sussex County. Because of this, the intimacy, trust, and openness of souls between Wicca Witches was absent, but Ash desperately attempted to reach out for a source of comfort in his loneness.

Through his studies, he perceived the universe and everything that was in it as a manifestation of the Divine. Ash sought a belief to guide him through the tribulations he was experiencing now. He perceived the philosophy of Wiccan belief to be the heart voicing the polarity of the Divine, where both male and female deities were honored. The Divine was the highest authority in a world that contained so many artificial values. The heart was the truest guide in life. Following the heart created an existence that was vibrant, responsive, spontaneous, and soulfull. Ash yearned to belong and freely follow his life without ridicule. He hoped Wicca would provide this.

This ceremony would require focus and limited movement. Ash was ready to begin creating the Circle.

He spread his Internet notes on the floor for reference.

Facing north, Ash knelt in front of the altar where he carefully placed the bowls of water and salt. Dipping the athame in the water, he quietly recited: "I exorcise thee, O Creature of Water that thou cast out from thee all impurities and uncleanliness of the world of phantasm, in the names of Cernunnos and Aradia."

In the cool night, small clouds of condensation accompanied his words, adding more mysticism to the ritual. Referencing his notes, he placed the athame in the salt: "Blessings be upon this Creature of Salt, let all malignity and hindrance be cast forth hence, and let all good enter herein, wherefore so I bless thee, that thou mayest aid me, in the names of Cernunnos and Aradia."

After pouring the salt into the bowl of water, Ash drew a clockwise circle in the air with the athame, trying to visualizing the power flowing into the Circle from the end of the knife. Checking his notes, he continued.

"I conjure thee, O Circle of Power, that thou bestow a meeting place of love and joy and truth, a shield against all wickedness and evil, a boundary between men and the realms of the Mighty Ones, a rampart and protection that shall preserve and contain the power that I shall raise within thee. Wherefore, I do bless thee and consecrate thee, in the names of Cernunnos and Aradia."

Ash sketched the Invoking Pentagram of Earth in the air with the athame. Facing the south he continued the summoning: "Ye Lords of the Watchtowers of the south, ye Lords of Fire, I do summon, stir, and call you up to witness this rite and to guard the Circle."

Facing west, he added, "Ye Lords of the Watchtowers of the west, ye Lords of Water, ye Lords of Death and Initiation, I do summon, stir, and call you up to witness this rite and to guard the Circle."

Facing east, he said, "Ye Lords of the Watchtowers of the north, ye Lords of Earth—Boreas, thou gentle guardian of the Northern Portals, thou powerful God and gentle Goddess, I do summon, stir, and call you up to witness this rite and to guard the Circle."

The Circle was completed. Ash depicted a pentagram with chalk in the middle of the circle.

Facing what he thought was the east, standing with his weight equally distributed on both legs, he imagined himself being microscopic, surrounded by all of the things which encircled him before. He opened himself to the adoration of the God who carefully and slowly developed him back to normal size, but the growing shouldn't stop. Ash tried to free his expansion until he could extend beyond the room and stand at top of the world.

Out of billions of stars visible through the roof hole, Ash focused on one star in particular and pointed his athame at it. He imaged other stars disappearing as this one's luminosity moved toward him, toward his athame. The energy of the silvery light fused into the blade. Ash placed the knife on his forehead and deeply chanted, "Ah-teh," and felt the sound of the word, the reverberations fill him, inside and out. He moved the athame to his genitals and uttered, "Malkuth."

Ash stood in the center of the Circle, with his arms outstretched in the form of a cross, moved his notes with his foot to the proper citation, and recited. "Before me stands Raphael, behind me Gabriel. At my right hand Michael, at my left hand Uriel. Before me flames the pentagram, and above me shines the six-rayed star."

Ash picked up a page and splayed his arms forward,

his voice stronger, more assertive. Reading for accuracy, he chanted. "*Eko, Eko, Azarak, Eko, Eko, Zamilak, Eko, Eko, Cernunnos, Eko, Eko, Aradia. Eko, Eko, Azarak, Eko, Eko, Zamilak, Eko, Eko, Cernunnos, Bagabi laca bachabe, Lamac cahi achababe, Karelyos! Lmaca lamac bachalyos, Cabahagi sabalyos, Baryolas! Agoz atha cabyolas, Samahac atha famyolas, Hurrahya!*"

Finished, Ash sat crossed legged on the floor to meditate on what he wanted, what he needed, what his prayers would answer. The chill helped him to concentrate. He wished not to be apart, not to be alone.

He was always distinctive. It was not that he didn't fit in, the world was singular—Ash was incongruent in this environment. After an hour of thought and introspect, Ash offered thanks for who he was and what he would be, accepted his providence, and gave praise, "Hecate and Innana, I thank you for the wisdom you have bestowed, and am forever grateful for your teachings. I hope to walk down this path with you. Blessed Be."

He carefully wrapped the athame in the hand towel. He opened the snacks and, with a cake in his right hand, gave gratitude for sustenance, "I bless this food, fruit of the earth, body of the goddess. Great God and Goddess, holy Guardians of the quarters, I ask you to partake in this feasting with me, on this night. Blessed be."

With the tomato juice in his right hand, he added, "I bless this drink, holy nectar of the earth, life blood of existence. Great God and Goddess, holy Guardians of the quarters, I ask you to partake in this feasting with me, on this night. Blessed be."

His path appeared to be evident and constant. He tried to be comforted in his existence apart from others. This, at least, helped him to belong, no matter how superficial it might be.

Ash studied his hands and, beyond them, the room. Goth, Wiccan, what was he really? There should have been a coven here tonight—others to share with. He looked around the decaying room and, not for the first time, wondered if he was foolish. He ate and began to write in his diary before sleeping on the witch's table.

CHAPTER 4

Jay disliked Devil's Night. It seemed an invitation to create mischief and damage in a sanctioned format. Tonight he and the rest of the department were answering toilet papering, mailbox tipping, and car window soaping calls from irate citizens—the same who let their children roam this night unsupervised.

The Town Council tried several times to have a Mischief Night party at the volunteer firehouse, but teenagers never attended and used the distraction of the police to accomplish more trouble.

Halloween was a most dangerous time: children walking the streets begging, masks covering identities, and no supervision could lead to serious problems. Luckily, that had never happened in Hamburg. The Town was small enough for all to know each other and the borough didn't have sidewalks or street view buildings for any Halloween activities outside of town.

Jay and two others in patrol cars slowly drove through the town and neighborhoods, not expecting any trouble. These visual reminders of law enforcement should be enough to deter any blatant mischief. Later he would swing out to the castle and factory, not expecting to find anything. What could have been damaged had been years ago. Ghosts and memories couldn't be vandalized.

✆ゝℯゝ

Ash awoke from dreamless peace to the sounds of mumbles and scraps: others were in the park and close by. Shedding the sleeping bag and zipping up his jacket, he peered through the boards in the front window. Yes, people were there. He had thought that this part of the park was relatively safe. Climbing out the window, Ash hid behind a collapsing stone wall—implanted with a crippled, bent, one-armed rusted gingerbread man sign that had withstood years of abuse—and observed several figures coming up the hill, looking to fulfill Mischief Night by damaging, destroying, or defacing something—anything that remained undisturbed. Decades of abandonment, however, left little to do. The group was frustrated.

Half a thought formed in Ash's head: if they come nearer, I'll lead the band away from my sanctorum. Discovery now would be one more reason to torment him. And closer they came. Flashlights marked paths. In an attempt to make a ghoulish face and scare a female in the group, the lead member turned and placed the light under his chin, emitting a low moaning. The girl was unafraid, the others laughed in deference. Ash recognized the jokester—it was Jud Robinson.

"Let's go over there." One pointed to the gingerbread house. "I ain't never been there before."

The pack moved on toward Ash. He made a decision and crept twenty yards from the house. Standing, he called out, "Assholes!" and raced on shattered cobble stones. His plan ended there. He didn't know where to go, but the castle loomed ahead with its many rooms.

"Who was that?" Jud asked no one in particular. "Let's get 'em!"

The mob ran after Ash, happy to have something to do.

Ash reached the castle foundation and entered the dungeon through a broken iron gate. It was completely dark, but memory guided him over rubble to a corner supply closet. He heard the searchers outside, guessing where he might be hiding.

"Danny, you and Chad go upstairs. Arnie, you and Craig go downstairs. He has to be in there somewhere. Brenda and me will wait here in case he escapes."

"What do we do if we find him?"

"Call out, we'll all come."

The first two reached the basement entrance. "You go first, Craig."

"What? Are you chicken?"

"Well, I don't see you rushing in there."

Arnie pushed Craig through the dungeon gate.

"Use your flashlight. I'm right behind you."

Arnie cautiously entered the castle basement behind Craig. The sound of cracking bones resonated off eroding walls as he stepped on an atrophied squirrel.

"What was that?"

"A dried up dead animal."

"Christ, be careful, no telling what's down here."

Craig stopped. "Who do you think it is?"

"I don't know."

"Could be a bum."

"So what?"

Craig shrugged. "Could be dangerous. Why don't we tell Jud no one was here?"

"What? You want to lie to Jud?"

"Well, you get your ass up front here then."

Arnie stood still, uncertain what to do.

Huddled in the closed space, Ash felt his left foot cramping. As he adjusted his position, his monkey boot thumped against the door.

Craig shone the light in the direction of the noise. "Over there!"

Ash held his breath. Why didn't he run in the open? He was trapped now. This was a stupid mistake.

"I don't see nothing. Maybe it's another animal."

"Keep looking."

Arnie tripped into a damp box of flat gypsum pink elephants that once adorned the rails to the first floor spiral stairs. They broke loose and slid across the cement floor. He stumbled and fell. His flashlight rolled and stopped against a pile of rusted chains.

Arnie grabbed his bleeding elbow. "Shit! My arm!"

"Let me see."

"What do you know?"

"Fine, have it your way."

Ash used the distraction to bolt from the closet, but he had to cross in front of the flashlight beam to get to the multi-colored curved staircase leading to the main floor.

Craig stared at the retreating shape. "Damn, do you know who that was?"

"Jesus, I don't care. My arm hurts!"

"It was the homo."

"Who?"

"How many homos do you know? Korbin, the guy with the makeup that we always beat up."

"No shit!"

Craig cupped his hands to his mouth and shouted at the dungeon gate, "Jud, Jud, it's the creepy queer! He's coming up the stairs."

Upstairs, Chad and Danny heard the alarm through a

hole cut into the floor covered with a ball-shaped lattice structure to protect visitors while viewing the Castle dungeon below.

Ash took the steps two at time, not looking back, not looking forward, and ran into Chad.

Chad seized Korbin's shoulder, placed a foot in the back of Korbin's leg, and threw him to the floor. "Well, if it isn't gay boy."

Ash stared up at Chad and Danny. He tried to rise, but Danny kicked him in the stomach. "Stay where you are, faggot."

Jud and Brenda joined the group as Arnie and Chad made their way up the stairs.

"What have we here?" Jud placed his hands on his hips and positioned himself directly over Korbin. "What are you doing out tonight? Are you alone? Of course you are alone—who would be friends with you?"

"I'm bleeding because of him," Arnie complained and showed the cut to everyone with manly pride.

"Don't be a cry baby. But I expect to see Korbbie here cry any moment, boys. Now, just what are we going to do with you?"

"Let's beat the shit out of him! Look at my arm!"

"No, no I don't want to have any more police trouble. I have a better idea. Pick him up."

"Where we going?"

"To the car."

Danny and Arnie grabbed an arm and pulled Korbin

along like a rag doll as the group silently marched to the fence. Ash knew it was useless to yell for help. As they dragged him to the edge of the park, his boots left tracks in the not yet frozen dirt and grass.

The mob surged through a fence opening then past the mill offices to an old dirt access lane that ran above the river which was once used to power the mill. Remaining dams formed large pools of water. Jud's midnight blue '65 Ford Galaxie was parked around a bend, hidden from the main road, behind the once-busy mill warehouse. Korbin was manhandled into the car's trunk.

"We're we going now?"

"We're taking this creep out of town."

"What?"

"Taking him to High Point and let him walk back. Nobody's out there. He'll really be alone. And best of all, no marks or bruises and I bet his parents didn't know he was in the park so he won't tell no one. This will really show him we don't want his kind here."

"Great idea, Jud."

Everyone nodded, happy to please Jud. Brenda was silent. She didn't agree, but she didn't want to anger Jud either. Being his girl ensured her standing at school and she enjoyed that elevated position.

The Ford Galaxie drove fourteen miles north on Route 23 to Hankins Road running alongside the sixteen thousand acres comprising High Point State Park.

"Maybe Bigfoot will get him."

"What?"

"Maybe Bigfoot will get him."

"There ain't no such thing."

"I saw a TV show that was hunting Bigfoot here."

"Did they find anything?"

"No."

"There you are."

"But there could be. They say Vince and Dawn are missing. Maybe Bigfoot got 'em when they were parking."

"Someone was yanking your chain."

"It's awful quiet back there. Do you think he's suffocating?"

"Naw."

Ash tried not to think of the confines of the trunk. His arms were folded behind him, his legs bent and cramping. Above the hum of tires, he could decipher part of the conversation from the car interior: High Point, Bigfoot. What he did not know was what they would do to him at High Point or what Bigfoot had to do with it. The ride seemed very long. For the first time, he was truly scared of the bullies.

Jud stopped a half mile down the hard gravel Hankins Road, at a section that was raised four feet above the surrounding wetland. Below, hemlock, white pine, spruce, cedar, and other old-growth trees stretched dark branches toward the road, as if trying to capture anyone foolish enough to stray near. Rhododendron, mountain laurel, and shrubs fought to live among the trees and formed an almost impenetrable wall on the park's irregular boundary. Insects were quiet on this autumn night, disturbed by the intrusion. Private residents bordering the park were very few—the entrances to their dwellings were nearly hidden within the dense wood. Street lights were absent on the nearly forgotten tertiary road. When clouds covered the moon, darkness was immediate. It was an eerie place on this night.

"Get the flashlights," Jud commanded.

The trunk was opened. A frightened Ash was wrenched out and tossed on the ground. Everyone was allowed a kick or punch. In the heat of the moment, Jud forgot his previous caution as he watched each strike and heard the pain. He felt good and placed his arm around Brenda's shoulders then slid his hand down to knead her ass. Brenda leaned into Jud, knowing this was the price for being with him, for now at least. She looked away as Ash was pummeled.

Jud grinned. "Okay. Okay. Enough fun, boys. Get rid of 'em."

Chad and Arnie held Ash by his arms and legs and began to swing him like a canvas hammock. Ash was thrown and landed two feet from the road, rolled down the embankment, stopping when his head hit a tree and he passed out.

Beams of light pierced the night, revealing the inert body sprawled against a large willow.

"Think he's dead?" Brenda breathed out.

The others stared at the still body, now afraid of what they might have done.

Jud hid his fear, asserting his leadership. "So what if he is?"

"We—we should find out," Brenda whispered.

Jud playfully nudged her back. "Sure, babe, you go down and take a look."

"Stop it. I think you went too far this time."

Alarms circled Jud, but he tried to remain strong and sought approval. "Crap, he's worth shit! It was good, wasn't it, guys?"

All spiritedly agreed and patted each other's backs. Arnie leaned over the bank and spit. The saliva globule didn't come near the body, but the gesture was satisfying and partially made up for his discomfort.

They all piled into the car. Jud made a jackrabbit start, leaving a trail of powdered stone, the occupants pleased with their success at finding real mischief this Devil's Night.

෪෨෪

Time became nonexistent, memory a puzzle. Ash discovered sheets beneath him, not grass. He didn't know where he was or how long it had been since he had been in the Gingerbread House. The existing light seemed dif-fused and his thoughts were murky. His head throbbed to the point that thinking was difficult. Jud, High Point, and Bigfoot. Running. High Point and Bigfoot kept coming to the fore. Where was he now? A shadow approached. Bigfoot? Ash started to sit up to defend himself, but his aching body wouldn't allow it.

"I'm sorry," a timid voice said from outside his vision.

Bigfoot talks? Ash tried to concentrate in the direction of the voice. "What?"

"I thought you were a female. You know, the makeup and everything. I brought you here before discovering you were not. I thought you were delivered to me."

Ash couldn't recognize the cadence of speech or comprehend the meaning. He finally sat up. His jacket was open and his black sugar skull T-shirt pushed up to his neck. "Where am I?"

"Here, my house," the young man replied from behind a window drape.

"Where's that?"

"Here. Why do you wear makeup if you are a boy?"

"I'm different from everyone."

"Me too, me too!"

Ash looked around the room. It was dark, lit only by moon light. "Who are you? What's your name?"

"I don't know what I am. My name is Ephraim."

"I'm Ash. What happened?"

"I—I found you by the road. I walk along there in

the woods every night, hoping she'll come back."

Sliding his foot on the floor, Ash started to stand, but sat back in pain. Little of what this figure said made sense.

"You all right?" Ephraim asked.

"Yes, just hurting a little."

"How did you get there—in the ditch by the road?"

"Bullies beat me up and left me."

"Why?"

"They don't like me—like who I am."

Ephraim jumped up and down in shared empathy. "Yes, yes, I know!"

"Who are you?" Ash asked, confused by the odd reaction.

"Ephraim."

Ash thought his aching head and body were preventing him from phrasing his questions well. He started again. "Where am I?"

"Here."

"Yes, I know here. Where is here?"

"The house."

"Where is the house?"

"Here."

Ash gave up questioning and let the throbbing and soreness take over. Falling back, he descended into a restless sleep.

"Yes, yes. Sleep. Tomorrow we will speak again." The figure danced from behind the drape and stood outside the door, trying to assess the current situation.

Ash was a kindred soul, a pippin, and could be a friend, something Ephraim never had. Perhaps Ash could help find Angelina! Ephraim became excited, but he didn't know what to expect when Ash finally saw him. Long ago, when he was young, others had become frightened and run away—or worse, ran at him to destroy the terror they imagined. Ephraim entertained locking all the doors so Ash couldn't escape. He must be careful. A human friend. How delightful!

CHAPTER 5

Jay was near the end of his midnight patrol—just a drive by the castle and mill remained. It had turned out to be a quiet night.

He slowed down and used the spotlight to illuminate the park entrance and the castle in the distance. Nothing unusual.

The mill was dark—not even the flicker of a candle or weak glow of flashlights to indicate any activity. Jay pulled in the old dirt access road to turn around and head toward Route 23. He made a mental note to check the area completely the next day for the missing couple, in case they went there to have sex and something happened to them.

A thorough search of all their known haunts was required now that the sergeant began to suspect they didn't leave town on their own. But what could have happened?

∽∾∽

Since Halloween was on a Saturday, everyone expected trick-or-treaters to be out late. Children and some teenagers spent the day preparing by laying out store-bought costumes or finding old clothes in attics.

Concerned parents lectured about razors in apples, unwrapped candy, or candy that appeared to have been re-wrapped. Caution was given to bring all candy home for inspection. Warnings about entering a strange house if invited were strongly counseled. And despite these dire admonitions, parents allowed their children to venture out into the night. Zombies, ghosts, witches, hoboes, and the unknowable were in force, begging in the late afternoon.

Ash awoke late morning with a dull persistent headache, bruised ribs and abdomen. The surroundings were unfamiliar. He seemed to be in a dusty doll house. "Hello?"

No one answered.

It took an effort to sit up. Slowly, the past night came back: Jud and his gang interrupting his communion, running through the park, being captured, the beating, and the mysterious voice.

"Hello, are you there?" A memory shard flashed, "Are you there, Ephraim?"

From behind the door, Ephraim answered, "I'm leaving you breakfast."

Ash used the bed stand to rise and shuffled toward the door. Under faded Persian carpets floor boards creaked. Steadying himself on the cool glass door knob, he opened the door. Emptiness rushed in and enveloped him with sadness. No one was in the dark hall that spread from one end of the house to the other. On the worn plank floor were a white rose patterned porcelain bowl of oatmeal and cup of green tea. A silver spoon was buried in the offered meal.

Ash needed to discover where he was, but was still lightheaded so he slowly picked up the food and placed it on the bed stand. The porridge was warm and comforting. Ash felt safe, despite the sterile environment and his unseen host. It was only now that he checked for his wallet and Celtic crosses—all intact. His face had been washed and poorly bandaged. Gingerly touching his green and purple bruises, he smelled Vicks VapoRub for the first time. Whoever this person was intended no harm and tried to doctor his injuries.

Ash had to urinate. Shambling back to the door, he called out, "Hello? I have to go to the bathroom."

Silence.

Using the blue peacock-flocked-papered walls for support, Ash slowly headed down the hall, past closed rooms toward a down staircase, looking for a bathroom.

From below, Ephraim said, "The water closet is on your right by the stairs."

"Thanks. I need to talk with you."

Silence.

Ash peered at the floor below. No one was in sight.

Mild pain accompanied red tinged urination. Washing, Ash looked up to view any marks on his face. No mirror by the sink—no mirror in the room.

Holding on to the large wooden handrail, Ash took one step at a time. At the bottom, he faced double-hung entrance doors with four opaque glass panes. A six-foot brown grizzly bear rose in frozen terror guarding the doors, teeth bared, claws extended. To the left was another pair of doors with a tarnished brass doorknob. Dusty antelope, deer, and elk heads, eyes huge with the surprise of death, hung on the hall to his right. Pelts were spread along the wall on his left. A worn tan and red oriental carpet lined the passageway, which seemed to lead to the back of the house. Everything was decorated with dark oak paneling, molding, and trim. Daylight found its way into the house by slipping around closed curtains and under doorsills.

"Ephraim?"

Mouse-like noises came from a room toward the back. It was a kitchen. Seated away from the door looking out a window was a small figure with a large head either praying or asleep.

"Ephraim?"

"Yes."

Ash moved closer. "I want to thank you for your care."

"I hope you liked the porridge and brew. I have barnbrack as well."

"Yes, thank you, Ephraim," Ash said, and not knowing what barnbrack was, added, "and no thanks."

"Do you require any more skof?"

"Skof?"

A short arm pointed to the pantry.

"Uh, no, no. I'm all right." Ash had no idea of the intent. "Can we talk?"

Ephraim slowly turned from viewing the cemetery. Ash was startled, seeing a crooked face on a conical head with sparse blond hair tufting from the top and sides, then realized it was Halloween and forced a small laugh in relief. "I see you are ready."

"Ready?"

"To go out."

"Oh, I do not go out."

With a chill, Ash began to realize that Ephraim was not wearing Halloween attire. He involuntarily gasped and backed up. He couldn't help but stare at the misshapen head, facial scars, pointed ears, and twisted mouth.

Ephraim turned back around and seemed to shrink into himself.

Ash involuntarily took another step backward. "Ephraim?"

"It is an inherited gift from the father. I know I am hideous."

"I…I…" Ash stumbled for the right words. "I'm sorry."

"So am I."

Not knowing what to say, but trying to find another topic, Ash asked, "Where are your parents?"

"Left."

"Left?"

"They are dead. So is Uncle. Please forgive me if I am hard to understand. Words—words do not come easily through my mouth and I have not really had a conversation with anyone for a very long while."

"Oh, I'm sorry." *Damn it, why do I continue to say sorry?* "Do you—do you live here alone then?"

"Yes. My family was obsessed with Pooterism. Are you going to leave me now?"

"Well, I—I need to be home tonight."

"I knew it, I knew it! I thought you would not be a friend to a mar!" Ephraim started to beat the sides of his head and stamp his right foot.

Ash grew fearful as Ephraim became increasingly agitated. Ash didn't know if he should approach to comfort him or remain safe at a distance. He raised his hands and waved, palms out, to assuage Ephraim, or perhaps to hold him off. He was confused.

"No. Wait, wait. I can be your friend, but I live somewhere else."

"You will be my friend?"

"Sure. Yes. Yes. Sure."

"Oh thank you, thank you." Ephraim clapped his hands but remained with his back facing Ash. "I thought you would find me repugnant."

Ash gained control, remembering the Wiccan rule: Harm none. "Ephraim, everyone has worth and value."

"Everyone. Worth. Value."

Ash's initial trepidation continued to ease. "I didn't know anyone lived out here."

"We needed privacy. The family moved here for seclusion in nineteen and five from the United Kingdom because of our family affliction. It demonstrates itself rarely, but I was cursed with it. People are afraid of me. I stay here, doggoing."

"Is there anyone else?"

"I am apart. Sometimes I do feel the blue devils."

"How—how do you manage if you don't go out?"

Ephraim pointed to the kitchen phone.

Ash sensed the emptiness of the house and the forlorn attitude of the person hiding but remaining visible before him. "I want to thank you again for taking care of me. Listen, that's what friends are for, right? I want to be your friend, but it's a long hike back to town, so I better start now."

"I have an automobile. Do you want to view it?"

"You drive?"

"Yes. I drive around the property. Uncle taught me. I

know Latin and Greek and studied ornithology. I am not a juggins!"

"I didn't mean to insult you. Do you think you could take me to town?"

Ephraim shook his head. "I—I do not want to be seen. I know I am punk."

"Well, we could go at dusk. People will think you are just a trick or treater."

"Trick or treater?"

"I'll explain and, and I'll teach you about Wicca."

Ephraim faced Ash. "You are not afraid of me?"

Now composed, Ash looked directly at Ephraim. "Wicca teaches us of the equality of all. Everyone is welcomed."

CHAPTER 6

Halloween was an unusual time to move, but a transfer from Saint Clare's Hospital in Dover was time sensitive for Heather's father, Clark, since the chief of emergency medicine abruptly resigned at this Sussex borough location, leaving only one resident physician. Snow and cold meant a constantly full emergency room with hunting, snow blower, car, and skiing accidents; frost bite; broken limbs from icy falls; burns from wood stoves; and a raft of other pastoral mishaps from across the county and surrounding areas. One doctor couldn't handle it alone.

The move would mean a promotion to chief for Clark—a position he would have to wait for a long time to attain in Dover. Clark didn't want to travel any distances on rural roads with winter approaching, so he rented a tan two-story condo on Falcon Ridge Way South for the winter till he was permanently promoted. This also provided the time needed to search for an appropriate single-family house worthy of a doctor.

Heather, Luna to her Goth friends back home, was unhappy over the relocation as any teenager in the beginning of a new school year would be, especially during Halloween, an important Goth occasion, but she kept her aura clear and controlled her emotions.

For Luna, Wallkill Valley Regional High School sounded too bucolic. Football, soccer, cross country, wrestling, basketball, field hockey, skiing, and yes, cheerleading were the major activities—all jock oriented with the sensitivity of the farm animals that surrounded the school. Not one, in all of the students, could possibility care for the artistic or creative aspect of the soul. Introspection and reflectivity were probably nonexistent out here. At least there were Raven, Alaric, and Danika at Dover High to hang with, share, and commiserate. Here, country bumpkins would most likely roam the halls, showing off athletic letters as badges of pride. She doubted there was a Goth within miles of Hamburg.

Luna sat at the edge of her bed and took in the surroundings of her new bedroom: neutral walls, windows without blinds, bright lights—nothing that reflected who she really was, how she really felt. The dark side of individualism was absent. Luna resolutely continued unpacking, wondering where she would buy black lipstick, creeper shoes, arm gloves, and even appropriate T-shirts and stockings. Her father had brought her to an alien world—she had to retain her sense of self.

A tap on her bedroom door announced Luna's mother who stood outside the threshold twirling her black shoulder-length hair with her fingers, "Heather, are you all right?"

Luna sighed. "Yes, Mother. I'm so fine."

"I know this is difficult for you, but it is a tremendous opportunity for Dad."

"I'm okay."

"You're such a good daughter. I'm sure you'll find new friends and fit in."

Luna examined the darkly dressed person in the mirror. A streak of green flowed through black-dyed locks. Gray eye shadow accentuated lavender contact lenses. Brown blush highlighted her cheeks. Absently, she ran her hands over her budding breasts and along her sides as she turned in a three-quarters profile and studied the reflection. Sure, sure, she would fit in.

"Tomorrow we're going to the nine o'clock service at the Prince of Peace Lutheran Church. Your father will be coming in late tonight so we'll let him sleep in the morning."

Luna doubted she would find peace here. The days ahead were going to be formidable, but she trusted her inner strength to, once again, pull her through adversity.

⌘⌘⌘

Mischief Night had been uneventful. No calls, no apparent damage. Halloween should be uneventful as well. Jay sat at his desk rereading the Data Collection Guide from the FBI. As a ranking officer, he didn't have to go on patrol one Saturday per month.

The missing pair bothered him more and more each day. This was the biggest case he had to solve since joining the force, and he started to feel that maybe he wasn't up to it. But what troubled him more was the fact that the kids' families didn't seem to care where their children were. Even if they were of legal age, parents should be concerned. How could young people disappear and parents not care?

He reviewed the list of personal descriptors and his notes:

* Scars, Marks, Tattoos, and Other Characteristics—obtained*

* Jewelry Type—not known*

* Miscellaneous Data—clothing (not known), build, hair description—obtained*

* Male and Female Characteristics—obtained: date of birth, hair and eye color, skin tone*

Image—photos obtained, signatures not

Jay reread the information before him: existence reduced to paper and ink. Two lives summarized by forms and diagrams. Was life so fleeting? Where were these damn kids?

The file folder would have to sit another week before he could declare them truly missing.

CHAPTER 7

Ephraim removed a key chain from the outstretched paws of a standing gray squirrel on the kitchen counter.

"You have a lot of stuffed animals here."

"Yes, Uncle was intensely interested in taxidermy. It is quite fun. He taught me so much. It is a very artistic craft. I will show you sometime. Would you like that, Ash?"

Ash tried to hide the uneasiness he felt. "Oh, okay."

"Come, pad the hoof with me." Ephraim was delighted about imparting his knowledge and excited about showing Ash the automobile.

"Do you have paper and pen?"

"Most certainly."

Ash pocketed the pad and pencil and followed Ephraim's irregular gate across the overgrown lawn to the barn. Ephraim skipped around him, pleased to have someone to talk with, pleased to have someone who had accepted him. Ephraim was wearing a gray wool frock coat that had been roughly cut with scissors in an attempt to make it fit him. The hem scraped the ground and scattered leaves. Shoulder pads drooped and the coat hung loose—he appeared lost within it.

"It is in there. I have not been in the barn for a while. I have been busy."

Ash half listened, trying to create a reasonable story that his parents would buy about his bruises.

"I believe the motor still turns, though I cannot be certain."

The barn wood was weathered to a brown-black color. Two huge double doors graced the front. An open rusted lock dangled useless on a hasp. The inside was damp and as cheerless as the late October day outside. Large and small dead birds, fastened to joists by nylon cord, swayed in the draft created by the intrusion as their outspread spread wings caught gusts of cool autumn air.

"Here, here." Ephraim pranced to a wall and turned a switch. A large single Edison light bulb hanging from the roughhewn center rafter started to glow.

"This is it. This is it." Ephraim pulled off a green canvas, revealing a Firemist Charcoal four-door Buick Regal sedan with black tinted windows.

"Wow!" Ash stared at the sixteen-and-one-half-foot automobile.

"Yes, yes, wow indeed. It is quite the automobile, is it not?" Ephraim was pleased with Ash's reaction. "Look, look."

He opened the door to reveal a silver Madrid interior with wood trim vinyl, a gray center console, three-speed automatic transmission, and faux-leather-wrapped steering wheel. Two cloth pillows were stacked on the driver's seat.

"You drive this?"

"Unquestionably. It is admirable fun. Get in. Get in." Ephraim climbed into the driver's side. "Get in Ash."

Blocks had been attached to the gas and brake pedals to accommodate him. The Regal started on the first try and rocketed out of the barn, leaving a blue cloud of exhaust behind.

Ahead, the old gray Edwardian house ascended from the fallow land like a broken tooth. Ephraim raced ahead. For a moment, Ash visualized crashing into the kitchen, but Ephraim careened down the drive, turned right at a large oak. Leaves spewed behind the car and caused it to drift a little. He turned right to the backyard then on to the driveway again.

Ash was pushed back against the seat and held onto the sides, his eyes open wide as the car skidded to a stop.

"Whoa, whoa!"

"See, see? I can drive, Ash!"

"Yes you can, but you will need to go slower on the road."

"Road?"

"You said you'd take me to town, Ephraim."

"I did?"

"Yes."

"Now?"

"It's getting dark and with the tinted windows on a Halloween night, you'll be all right."

"Halloween. Yes. People dress to become like me."

"We talked about that remember?"

"I think so."

Ash checked the gas gauge—it pointed to half full. "When you need more gas, go to Pennsylvania. It's near-by. You can pump gas by yourself at night, not like here in New Jersey where there are attendants. No one will see you."

"Will I see you again, Ash? Are you going to leave me, too?"

"We exchanged telephone numbers. You can call me and I'll call you. I'm your friend now Ephraim."

"You are my friend?"

"I am."

"Friend!" A smile appeared on Ephraim's twisted mouth. The Regal started to move at a slow pace. "I have never been off our property. It was not allowed."

"Don't worry, I'll write down directions as we go so you can get back."

The car stopped before an invisible barrier at the front gate. Ephraim had never been beyond this point—he did not want to go farther.

"What's the matter?"

"I only come here to get the post and I reach for it through the gate."

"You don't open it?"

"I open it from inside the house. I do not know how to open it here."

Ash got out, inspected the gate, and returned. "It's electronic."

"I guess you will have to stay then, Ash."

∽∾∽

Jud had spent the last two months trying to convince Brenda to give it up, as this was the price for being with him. The time had passed when fleeting feels through her blouse and open-mouth kissing would do. Besides, everyone already thought they were having sex. If she didn't want to take the relationship further, there were other girls who would. Lately, Brenda appeared to be enthusiastic and she hadn't said no to his hints. She had been giving him signs that he read as promising—she was ready. Jud decided that tonight was the night.

The Ford was packed with blankets and a pillow. Jud's pocket was stuffed with three Trojans and a roll of breath mints. Wicked Game by Chris Isaak was set to play in the recently installed CD player—talk around school was that this was the best song ever to get a girl in the mood. Jud was ready. Brenda had better be ready too.

Brenda lived on Bluffs Court in a gray colonial in the Fairways at Wallkill River just past the old Wheatsworth Mill and Gingerbread Castle. On their last date, Jud had told Brenda's parents they would be going to a Halloween party tonight.

Hiding a smirk, Jud politely greeted Brenda's father, Mr. Armstead. If only he knew what was going to happen to his daughter tonight and so close to home!

Paul nodded and let Jud step into the living room. "Have a seat."

"Thank you, sir." Jud zipped open his leather jacket, absentmindedly patted his blond hair in place, and automatically showed his signature smile. He positioned himself on a Trent leather chair to highlight his six-foot-two-inch athletic frame, unaware that it was Mr. Armstead's favorite resting place. Paul retrieved *The Advertiser News* from the end table by the Trent and sat on the sofa. He made an exaggerated gesture opening the newspaper to show his displeasure and unnecessarily adjusted his wired-rimmed glasses. Jud didn't notice.

Paul had never liked Jud and hoped this friendship was a temporary thing. Brenda could do a lot better and would hopefully find someone more to her level at college.

Brenda's mother, June, came to greet Jud. Jud rose

and gently took her free hand. "It's always a pleasure to see you, ma'am."

June almost blushed. Jud was the type of boy she wished she had attracted in high school. Brenda was so lucky. She held out an appetizer plate, "Have some banana bread, baked fresh."

"Thank you." Jud took a piece and ate it whole, then grabbed another. "You are such a fine cook, Mrs. Armstead."

This time, June did blush and tried to recover, "Why aren't you dressed up for the Halloween party tonight, Jud?"

"Costumes are for children, Mrs. Armstead. This is more of a social event."

Yes, of course." June became embarrassed over her assumption. She looked down, rubbed her hands at her side, and then acted to move beyond her obvious gaffe by calling up to her daughter, "Brenda, Jud is here."

She put the plate down on the coffee table, went to the steps, and grabbed the banister, as if it would produce Brenda. Jud noticed June's reaction and was pleased. He had a charm that worked on women of all ages.

Brenda appeared at the top of the stairs and paused for effect. She was wearing a Charlotte Russel pink chiffon blouse, a thigh-length black Ibex skirt, and opaque Diana cotton tights that accentuated her slim legs. Her feet sported UGG boots. Auburn hair was brushed to a sheen and fell about her shoulders.

Jud's smile grew wider. He moved to the stairs. "She looks just like you, Mrs. Armstead."

June blushed again as Jud touched her back.

Paul rustled the newspaper in his lap and stared at the performance, his annoyance with June and his growing dislike of Jud increasing.

Brenda floated down the steps. "I'm ready."

Yes, you are, Jud mused. "Don't worry, we'll be back early," he assured June.

"You kids have fun."

Brenda took a Michael Kors charcoal scarf and fur-trimmed hooded wool coat from the hall closet. Jud helped her put them on.

"We'll be home early, Mrs. Armstead," he repeated.

June beamed at the politeness of the boy and his attention to her daughter. Paul watched as they entered the blue Galaxie then returned to his newspaper, happy that Jud finally left so he could regain his chair.

Jud opened the passenger door for Brenda, in case June was watching. He turned on the CD. A smooth guitar melody with silky sensual vocals fills the interior.

"Where's the party?" Brenda inquired.

"Just up the road."

Brenda was confused, but didn't want to challenge Jud.

The Ford bore right into the mill access lane.

"What's this?"

"It's where the party is."

"Here?"

"Oh, yeah!"

"I don't understand."

Jud turned left into an area by the loading docks, the river behind the car and almost blocked from street view by the building. He faced Brenda, who looked quizzical.

"We're not going to the castle again, are we?" she asked.

"No, no we're staying right here."

"I still don't understand."

Jud reached over, slipped the scarf from her neck, and dropped it at her feet. Brenda's hands covered her exposed neck.

"What are you doing?"

"What we should have done a while ago."

He started to undo her coat.

"Wait, wait. I'm not ready."

"I am." Jud massaged her left breast through her blouse and leaned over for a kiss.

Brenda squirmed as he closed in. "Jud!"

"Easy, easy," Jud breathed. He grasped her legs and placed them behind him on the seat. "I've thought of everything just for you." He reached to the back and produced the pillow. "For your comfort!"

Brenda clasped her knees tightly together. "No. No, not now."

"Don't continue to be a tease—time to give it up, Brenda! You'll enjoy it, believe me."

"No, not like this!" Brenda struggled to find the car door handle behind her. She backed against the door trying to escape. "Stop it! Stop it! I'm not ready."

Jud ignored her pleas as his excitement increased. He threw the pillow back, grasped the seat back for support, and straddled above her, trying to force her legs open with his left hand.

"Get your f-ing hands off of me Jud!"

He slipped on her silk stockings and his elbow hit the horn. The sharp noise startled them both then Jud went back to work.

℘℘℘

Ash sat quietly thinking, alongside a grinning Ephraim. "Did your parents use the car?"

"Most certainly."

"How did they get past the gate?"

"I do not know."

"Do you open the gate from the house?"

"Yes, to permit the delivery of parcels and skof."

Then it dawned on Ash: of course, so simple, like a garage door opener. He opened the glove box and dug around finally retrieving a remote device. The gate swung open. The grin disappeared from Ephraim's face.

"What is that contraption?"

"It's a remote. You can open the gate from anywhere on the property. Okay, let's go."

The car didn't move.

"Ephraim?"

"I do not want you to leave."

"I have to go to my house. But I'll be in touch with you. Remember, you have my phone number as well. Trust me."

Ephraim looked directly at Ash—the first time in his life that he had faced another person other than Uncle. He thought then decided, "Yes, I will trust you Ash."

"Good. Turn left after the gate. I think that's the way home."

The car jumped to a start. Ash closed the gate behind them. They travel north along Hankins Road, then on Route 443, through Colesville as 443 become Route 23.

"It's easy to get back. I wrote the directions down. Now turn right onto Gingerbread Castle Road. I need to pick up my things. Stop here."

Ephraim braked at the castle entrance.

He looked at the ruins: much like his house, only colorful. "You live here?"

"No. I live a few blocks away."

"Why have we stopped here then?"

"I was studying in one of the buildings and left my books there."

"We will then go to your house?"

"No, I'll walk from here."

"Oh."

"I am your friend, Ephraim. I will call you. You can

turn the car around in the road on the left after the mill and then follow my directions. Understand?"

"Yes, Ash, I do."

"Okay. See you later."

"See you later, Ash."

Ephraim watched Ash withdraw into the overgrowth. He sat for a while looking around at this wild outside world. It wasn't too different from the view of his backyard. The castle held the same loneliness and sadness that was trapped inside his house. Perhaps there were more like him as well. Perhaps he was not so different after all.

Ephraim slowly continued down the road to an opening on his left and entered the access lane. His foot slipped off the brake blocks and he traveled farther into the lane than he wanted to go. Slightly unnerved, he turned the car off to gain composure. This was the first time he was by himself outside his secure confines. Ephraim searched for the directions Ash wrote down. He studied and memorized the path to home. As the silence settled around him, a high-pitched noise arose from farther on.

Ephraim huddled down, afraid someone was near. Nothing happened—he seemed to be alone, but curiosity again compelled him to action. He clambered out of the car to investigate.

The empty building on his left was dark, but comforting in its isolation. Hobbling forward over the rutted road, he spotted something reflecting the moon light. It appeared to be a trunk of a car barely visible behind another building.

Soothing sounds of the Wallkill River on his right mixed with the muffled tune of a song from within the car ahead. Interspersed, however, were cries. Memories of Angelina rushed forward. The car was rocking, just like before. Ephraim hurried forward, not daring to hope that Angelina had returned.

☙❧❦

Ash stuffed his possessions into the knapsack and sleeping bag. He wiped out the chalk pentagram as best he could. Jud and his crew might return to find out why he was in the park. He needed to find a new sanctorum and Ephraim's house might be the answer. Almost finished, Ash froze as he heard a car horn. *Are they back?* He looked out the window and waited to see beams of light, but there was nothing unusual. He erased any traces of his being here and started for home.

Ash remained one block away from his house till the latest trick-or-treaters left. When no others were in sight, he walked briskly across the lawn and slowly opened the front door.

The living room was empty, but half way up the stairs his mother called from the kitchen. "Korbin, is that you?"

"Yes, Mother." Ash bolted upstairs to hide his stuff.

"Korbin, come down here and speak to your parents."

"Just a minute." Ash quickly looked in the mirror. The swelling hadn't gone down much: black, green, and purple bruises were all over his face. Pain remained, if slightly dulled.

There was nothing he could do about it now. He gradually descended, rehearsing his story.

"How was your night, dear?" Dorothy saw her son's face. "Korbin, Korbin! What happened? Henry, Henry, come look at your son. Quick! Oh dear, oh dear!" Dorothy rushed close to Korbin and placed her hands near his face, afraid actually to touch it. "My baby, my baby!"

Korbin retreated from the smothering of his mother. "I'm all right."

"Henry, get in here now!"

Korbin's father arrived from his study. "Wow! What happened, son?"

"I saw some guys stealing candy from trick-or-treaters and I tried to stop it. There were too many of them."

Dorothy didn't know what to do beside fret. "Oh, oh, Korbin!"

"Doesn't look good." Henry inspected Korbin by gripping his chin between his thumb and index finger, turned Korbin's face right then left. Parts were puffy, the color of rotten vegetables. His swollen nose had a broad band of red near the eyes, indicating a possible break.

"Get your coat—we're going to the emergency room."

"I'll be fine."

"Put your coat on!"

Korbin returned to his room to retrieve his jacket. He studied the mirror again. Outwardly, the image staring back was difficult to recognize with the swelling and contusions. His hair was unkempt and his mascara had faded. He hardly recognized himself, but he knew who he was and that was the important thing.

"Korbin!"

"Okay, okay, I'm coming."

"I'll come too!" Dorothy turned around and around, trying to locate the hall closet in her parental turmoil.

"You stay here. You're not in the mood to do any good."

"I need to come. Where's my coat?"

"I'll phone you from the hospital with information."

"He's hurt, Henry, he needs his mother." Dorothy twirled faster now, forgetting her coat, now looking for her purse.

Henry took a hold of her shoulders and sat her down. "I'll call you. Don't get so excited. Calm down, it's not that bad. It will be all right. Okay? It will be all right!"

Dorothy placed her hands on her lap and breathed deeply.

"That's it. Relax. He's not in danger." Henry tightened his green necktie, put on a tweed three-button wool coat, and retrieved the car keys from on the door stand.

He tried not to interrogate Korbin on the ride to Saint Clare's. There would be plenty of time later for inquiries. Inwardly, he was proud of Korbin for standing up to bullies.

From Route 23, Henry turned onto Fourth Street and then two blocks onto Walnut Street. The compact thirty-bed brick hospital came into view. The building was fairly new—the pain and sorrow within was not.

He followed bright red signs to the emergency room entrance. Henry thought about helping Korbin out, but decided against it, not wanting to seem as doting as Dorothy.

Inside, he ushered Korbin to the recessed registration desk and was told by a petite young woman to sit in the waiting room for a triage nurse.

After fifteen minutes, a middle-aged nurse approached, clipboard in hand. She introduced herself as Nancy and positioned herself on a pale green plastic chair next to Korbin. Nancy began to record his vital signs: temperature, heart rate, blood pressure, and breathing, concluding that nothing about Korbin's injuries were life threatening. She gave Henry a yellow plastic tag with a black number on it: twenty-four. Henry surveyed the room. It was packed with ailing people, some with homemade arm slings, others with ice bags resting on limbs, a few with crutches, and several in costumes that complemented their injuries.

Nancy addressed Henry, "Your number will be

called. You can then register." She disappeared down a hall.

Henry cleared his throat, "You all right, son?"

"Yes I'm okay."

Henry folded his arms, stared at a subdued pink and white watercolor of lilies on the wall in front of him, and waited, secretly stealing looks at Korbin.

Ash watched the helpless people around him.

An hour passed. Henry had kept Dorothy current every thirty minutes.

"Number twenty-four," a disconnected voice called through a ceiling speaker.

"That's us." Henry led Korbin to the registration desk again.

"Please follow me."

The young woman walked ahead. Both Henry and Korbin focused on her swaying hips. He became very conscious of his beaten face and the weak image he must be projecting.

Realizing this, Henry tried to bolster Korbin. "My son here is a hero, miss. He saved some children from being roughed up by a mob of teenagers."

The woman stopped, turned, and seemed to appraise Korbin. "Really? That's very admirable."

Portions of Korbin's face blushed from her attention and because he hadn't heard a compliment from his father in a long while.

"In here, please." The woman indicated two worn

chairs in front of a laminate desk. "I need some information before a doctor will see you."

"Will this take long?"

"No, but it's necessary."

She asked and wrote down answers about current medications, allergies, surgeries, telephone number, address, social security number, pharmacy, and insurance coverage then directed them back to the still full waiting room.

"This isn't necessary. I feel fine."

"It doesn't hurt to be thorough, Korbin."

Another fifteen minutes passed before the receptionist waved to a man wearing a white lab coat and pointed toward them.

"Good evening. I'm Doctor Clark Brenson, acting chief of emergency medicine. I'm sorry for the wait. We've had quite a full house and only one resident physician. Halloween is usually busy with pedestrian collisions, eye injuries from sharp masks, burns from flammable costumes, falls, and the like. Please come with me."

Doctor Brenson led them to a small sterile examination room.

White paper crackled as Korbin sat at the end of an exam table. He tried to remain still.

Brenson reviewed the information attached on a clipboard. "All right. Suppose you tell me what happened."

Henry started to speak.

"I'd rather hear it from Korbin."

Korbin looked from his father to the doctor then cleared his throat. "Well, I saw a bunch of guys harassing some small kids. I imagine it was for the candy. I stepped in to protect them and got beat up."

"When did this happen?"

"Tonight."

"Tonight huh?"

"Yes."

"Okay. Let me take a look." Brenson shined a light in Korbin's eyes. "Now, please follow my finger." Slowly he moves it from left to right then back. "Were you unconscious?"

"No."

Brenson looked Korbin directly in his eyes and saw anxiety. He faced Henry. "Mr. Miller would you please wait outside the room so I can finish my examination?"

"What?"

"Protocol, Mr. Miller."

Henry hesitated then bowed to authority. "I'll be right outside, Korbin."

After the door closed, Brenson addressed Korbin. "Now, you want to tell me what really happened?"

Ash remained silent looking at the floor.

Doctor Brenson waited him out.

Finally, Ash said. "I was beat up."

"That I can see."

"Some seniors beat me because of who I am."

"Who are you?"

"An independent. Different. I'm a Goth."

"That would explain the mascara."

"There's nothing—"

Doctor Brenson cast his eyes down with a resigned expression. "I know, I know, my daughter is a Goth."

"Your daughter?" Ash was alert and leaned forward. Perhaps his prayers were answered. A kindred soul and a female to boot. He was not alone. Could she also be a Wiccan?

"Heather, but she calls herself Luna."

"I'm Ash. I haven't seen her around."

"We just moved here yesterday."

"How old is she?"

"About your age, seventeen."

"I'm the only Goth around here."

Brenson visibly brightened at this news.

Ash wanted more information about Luna, but didn't know how to directly ask. "I could show her around the school."

Dr. Brenson ignored the remark. Perhaps he didn't approve of his daughter's choices. "Now, truthfully, were you unconscious?"

Ash hesitated, not knowing if the doctor could diagnose unconsciousness. "Yes."

"For how long?"

"I don't remember."

"Do you feel confused?"

"No."

"Any memory loss?"

"No."

"Drowsiness, sluggish feeling?"

"No."

"Dizziness, blurred vision?"

"No."

"Nausea or vomiting?"

"No."

"Headache?"

"Initially, but it's gone now."

"How severe?"

"Mild."

"Let me look at your nose." Brenson pinched the bridge of Korbin's nose. "Hurt?"

"Hurt? No, but sore yes."

"Any bleeding?"

"No."

"Can you breathe all right—nose isn't stuffy?"

"I breathe fine."

"Any other bruises?"

Korbin pulled up his shirt to reveal marks on his sides and abdomen.

The doctor pressed each area. "Pain?"

"Not really, just sore."

"Would you give me the name of these seniors if I asked?"

"No."

"So you don't know them."

"Yes."

"I have to report this to the police, but since you can't identify the assailants, I doubt much will happen." Brenson opened the door. "You can come in now, Mr. Miller."

"Is everything all right, Doctor?"

"Yes, nothing to worry about. No broken retinas, or broken skin, but there are signs of a severe concussion. However, his eyes track well, so I am not overly concerned."

"Concussion?"

"Yes, he did black out and this constitutes the term, severe. You will need to monitor him till tomorrow."

"That's not dangerous?"

"We'll have to wait and see."

"How about his nose?"

"Not broken."

"Great! He's quite a hero, you know."

Brenson didn't look at Korbin. "Yes, for sure. Now here's what you can do, Mr. Miller. Apply ice to the nose for any lasting pain and swelling. Also apply a cold pack or ice wrapped in a wash cloth to the bruises. Give him acetaminophen for pain—that would be Tylenol. Do not give NSAIDS such as Advil, Motrin, or aspirin. I'll write this down."

"Thank you, Doctor."

"Schedule a visit with your primary as soon as possible."

Ash didn't speak to Brenson on his way out. He was thinking about Monday.

ᴄᴏᴄᴏ

Ephraim cautiously approached the Ford, his excitement growing and his thoughts racing. This was similar to the situation she came to him the last time. Angelina must be back and needed to be rescued yet again! He was up to it! Ash truly was his friend. If Ash hadn't asked him to leave the house, he might not have seen Angelina for a second time. He had waited so long in the swamp. Now, now thanks to Ash, Ephraim realized that he didn't need to wait for her to appear and could find her himself, if necessary.

Looking around in the moonlight, he picked up a brick and momentarily stopped by the trunk of the car. Through the back window, he saw Angelina struggling to get to him, desperate for him to save her. She pressed her back against the passenger door, trying to escape. He could hear her pleading, but couldn't understand the words. Surely, she was calling his name. He grabbed the door and pulled it open. Angelina half fell back, hitting the back of her head on the Ford's rocker panel. Golden-brown hair spilled over the dirt and rubble of the warehouse dock. Her legs remained inside. She didn't move.

A startled face stared at him from within. "What the hell! Holy shit! My god, what the hell are you?" Jud backed away from the small frightful figure, forgetting about Brenda.

Ephraim reached in, striking the blond head with the flat of the brick. Jud collapsed on the seat, his face between Angelina's calves resting on sheer stockings and panties that begin to turn red. Ephraim pulled Angelina completely out and climbed in. The brick swung again and again, till there was no longer a cracking noise, just a squishing sound.

The body was still. Ephraim didn't need to think, just remember his actions before. He dragged Angelina to his car and folded her onto the front seat. Her breathing was labored.

Returning to the Ford, he looked around and there it was—water. The car must go into the river with the body. Providentially, there were no trees on this side of the embankment. An unobstructed path led directly to a dammed portion of the river.

Ephraim partially closed the passenger door and opened the driver door. The shift was not like the Buick, but he recognized the letters. Moving the inert body, he slipped the car to N for neutral then shut the door. Summing up all his strength, Ephraim grabbed the front bumper and moved forward. Slowly, the car started to stir. Each labored step and push led closer to the bank. The rear wheels moved off the hard-packed dirt onto soft leaves and vegetation. The car stopped. Ephraim slumped on the road, exhausted.

He visualized bringing Angelina home again, stood, and leaned into the hood. Gradually, the Ford advanced with each labored short stride till gravity took control and the car rolled down toward the pool below. Ephraim watched the slow descent. The car halted at the edge. Ephraim became alarmed, but just as before the car progressively sank into the water. The river rushed in the open doors and filled the interior. This time it disappeared completely below the surface—an auspicious sign.

Ephraim threw the brick he still clutched through a pane-less window. He looked where the Ford had rolled down. In the dim night light, no traces of tire marks were visible. He returned to his car.

Angelina was moaning slightly. Her right breast was exposed and her disheveled skirt revealed her nakedness. Ephraim became aroused, but realized their pleasures would have to wait till they both were safe and alone.

Ephraim gripped the steering wheel and drove forward then made a sharp left into the dock lot to where the Ford had been parked.

Nearly standing to see out the back window, he guessed where the road and bank were, turned the wheel right, slowly reversed the big car back onto the road, then headed out.

At the end of the lane, he opened the glove box and

reread Ash's directions. Looking at Angelina, he lightly touched her nipple and shivered with anticipation.

"Soon, my love, soon."

CHAPTER 8

Twenty-four-year-old Ned Hines had pushed his rolling office chair against the paneled wall—his small feet were on the desk. No one was around and the corporal was taking advantage of the calm. Sundays were usually quiet at the police station. The heater in the corner had warmed the reception area and his thin body. Head against the paneling, he fell into a light sleep, but was awakened by the harsh ring of the black desk phone. Hines almost toppled over in his seat as he reached for the phone. He regained his composure as it rung one more time.

Ned cleared his throat to sound authoritative. "Good morning, Hamburg Police Station. How may I help you?" he asked in his best baritone tone. He stiffened as he listened to the call. Scrambling, he found a pad and pen and began to write. After ten minutes of reassuring the caller, he returned the hand phone receiver to its cradle. This was not good. Not good at all. He reluctantly, but hurriedly, called Sergeant Hurray at home.

"Sarge." His voice was now higher.

"Yes?"

"Sorry to bother you on your day off, but another young couple is missing."

"What?"

"A Paul Armstead called. His daughter, Brenda, didn't come home last night."

"You said couple."

"Yes. She was out on a date with Jud Robinson. June, Brenda's mother, called the Robinson house and he hasn't returned either. Since you had the previous missing persons case, I thought you should know immediately."

"Damn it! How old are they?"

"Seventeen."

"Well, this means an amber alert."

"Oh, and the hospital called about a gang mugging. A teenager was pretty beat up. Maybe they're related."

"This gets better and better. I'm coming in."

☙⋙⋘❧

Jay returned to the kitchen and folded the open Sunday paper left on the table. Addressing his wife and children, he said, "I need to go to the station."

"Anything important? You look worried."

"No, no, just some procedures that need to be worked out."

"Today? What about breakfast? When will you be home?"

"I'll get something on the way. I probably won't be home for lunch. I'll try to make it for dinner. I'll call."

"This is your day off. It's not fair. What could be so important?"

"It's my job, dear."

Arriving at the station, Jay remained in his car, not ready to get out and face what could be a long day ahead. Could these missing adolescents be part of a pattern? How would the town react? What more could he do? His mind was reeling as he entered the building. He forgot about the mugging.

"Sarge! Glad you're here."

"I bet you are, Hines. Fill me in."

Hines shrugged. "Not much more than what I told you over the phone."

"Did either of the missing know the Marconi boy or Dawn Portny?"

"Don't know that."

"Did you talk with the Robinsons?"

"No."

"Jesus, Hines, what *did* you do?"

"Answered the phone. I know this is your case."

"Damn it, Corporal, I know the first missing reports are mine, but this is all our case now."

"Yes, sir."

"Issue an amber alert for the two."

Jay took the initial report from Hines and went to his desk. Slumping in his seat, he retrieved the Marconi/Portny folder from the top drawer. There must be something to link the two cases for them to have happened in such a short amount of time. Jay started to fill out the National Crime Information Center initial Entry Report, comparing this one to the previous. There had to be a link, a significant similarity to help solve these cases. He again reminded himself to see the optometrist as he moved the papers into focus.

On a notepad, he created two columns summarizing what he had so far: Similar and Different.

Similar

Juvenile (EMJ): category

Residents of Hamburg

Both are couples

Attended Wallkill Valley Regional

Males owned automobiles

No distinguishing marks

Different

Not known to each other

> *Different circle of friends*
> *No same activities*
> *Different neighborhoods*
> *Parental attitudes*

Not much tangible information. He gathered the folder, a pad, and the new NCIC Initial Entry Report and set out to see the Armsteads. He turned on Gingerbread Castle Road and onto Bluffs Court.

June Armstead opened the door before he could knock.

"Officer, any news?"

She was distraught and looked directly into his eyes as if this would produce a satisfactory answer.

"No news, Mrs. Armstead. It's still early. She might show up anytime." Jay knew this wasn't true, but the woman desperately needed some reassurance. "May I come in and ask you some questions?"

"Certainly, please, please. Paul, Paul, the police are here."

Paul rushed in with expectations, with hope.

"Please sit here." June indicated the sofa to the sergeant. "Would the kitchen table be better? Of course, it would be. Something for you to write on. Would you like a cup of coffee? Perhaps tea?"

"Calm down, June." Paul placed his hand on her shoulder. "Sit and let the sergeant do his work."

"Yes, yes, of course."

Jay opened his folder to the NCIC report. "There are questions I need to ask for procedural matters. In themselves, they don't mean anything. Understand?" He looked at a very flustered June and smiled, hoping to calm her.

June wrung her hands and nodded repeatedly. Paul shifted unable to stand still.

The sergeant asked the same questions he put forth to the Marconi and Portny parents, writing the answers in the form. "Did either of you attempt to call Brenda on her cell phone?"

"Yes, several times, but she doesn't answer, and that's not like her, Officer, not at all." June replied. "I left messages. She always answers. Brenda is a polite, considerate girl, always courteous. Isn't that right, Paul?"

Paul continued to pat her shoulder. "Yes, dear."

"What is the address of the Halloween party?"

June appeared vacant.

"Ah, we don't know," Paul finally answered. "We never thought to ask. We trusted Jud and this is such a safe community."

"Can I have a list of her friends?"

"Certainly, certainly, we can do that." Paul looked at June for confirmation.

"One more question. Did Brenda know Vincent Marconi or Dawn Portny?"

"I don't recognize the names. Do you honey?" Paul asked June.

"No, no. Who are they? Are they somehow involved?"

"Not that I know of, ma'am. Just checking all possibilities."

June took a tight hold of Paul's arm to brace herself. "Do you think something bad has happened, Officer?"

"No, no, Mrs. Armstead, just being thorough."

June relaxed for only a moment. "You will keep us informed?"

"Of course."

"I mean even if it is bad news. Tell us immediately."

"Yes, yes, I will."

"Any news. You can't imagine how we feel. This is not like Brenda, and we fear the worst has happened. We pray to Jesus it has not."

Jay left before they could ask any more questions. He was thankful that Paul was present. June seemed on the edge of a breakdown. Jay headed out to the Robinsons on Card Street off Route 94.

Bud Robinson greeted Jay. "Come in. You know, I don't think there is much to this. Jud mentioned he was going to a Halloween party and probably slept over."

"Do you know where the party was?"

"No, not exactly. Probably at one of his buddies' house."

"Who would that be?"

"He has a lot of friends, Danny, Chad, Arnie, Craig. Could be any one of them."

"You don't know?"

"Listen, Sergeant, Jud is a responsible person, a good student, active in athletics, someone a father can be proud of. I don't micromanage him."

Jay had heard this before. "Can I have the last names of his friends?"

"Let's see, Danny Calvan, Arnie Mente…hum, ah…Allyson, could you come in here?"

"What's the matter?"

"This is Sergeant…"

Jay stood. "Sergeant Hurray."

"He's here because of June Armistead's concern for Brenda. Do you know the last names of Jud's friends?"

"Have you information about Jud?"

"Not yet, Mrs. Robinson."

"Allyson, we need the names of Jud's friends to help track him down."

"Track him down? Has he run away?"

"No, not at all, Allyson. The police just need to locate him. The names please."

"Oh, yes, yes. Let's see, Craig Thomson, Danny Calvino, Arnold Mente, and Chad Ryan."

"Calvino?"

"Yes. Why do you need these names?"

"Your husband thinks Jud might be with them. Did you call Jud?"

"Why?"

"To find out where he is."

"June's a worry wart. I'm sure they are just fine." Bud winked at Jay and handed Allyson his cell phone.

Placing her hand over the device, she frowned. "No answer. It's not ringing and I don't get voice mail."

"He might be in an area that doesn't have cell phone service like the hills up north," Bud assured his wife.

"But who does he know there?"

"I don't know. It doesn't mean anything. Any more questions, Sergeant?"

Jay asked the questions on his list and recorded each answer—a little more information than the Marconi visit. "Thank you." He departed without much to go on. In the car, he gave Hines a call. "Ned, get me the addresses and phone numbers for these names and have everyone look out for a midnight blue '65 Ford Galaxie."

Parking down the street, he waited for Hines to get back to him. Ten minutes later, Hines supplied the information. Jay called each to determine if Jud was there and advised he would be stopping by to ask some questions.

After four hours of interviews produced nothing new, the sergeant returned to headquarters. Hines was going off duty.

"Find anything?"

"No, and no association with Marconi or Portny." Jay retreated to his desk to follow up on the Amber Alert process and complete the new NCIC report.

CHAPTER 9

Ephraim hurried home, careful to follow Ash's directions. Angelina was stirring beside him. He became alarmed as she cried out and thrashed weakly.

The gate was closed. Ephraim searched the glove box and found the remote. He turned it around in his hand before finally pressing a button. The gate swung open, almost hitting the car. The barn light welcomed him home. The Buick Regal glided over leaves and stopped by the side kitchen door. Ephraim exited and hobbled into the house to turn on the interior lights. He returned and grabbed Angelina under the arms then, walking backward, maneuvered her through the kitchen and, with minimal effort, upstairs. Her feet struck each riser, finally causing her right boot to come off. It flipped and tumbled almost to the bottom. Ephraim reached the third bedroom on the floor. The room was dusty, stale, and dim with only pale moonlight filtering through old cotton curtains.

Pushing her up onto the high four-poster bed, Ephraim stepped back and admired her loveliness. Still dazed, Angelina tried to sit up. Ephraim mistook her action for eagerness and unbuckled his belt. He was hard. He removed his blood soaked coat and pants. Excitedly he took off her skirt, soiled panties and stockings. He clambered on top of the bed and above her. She was as beautiful as he remembered. Ephraim slowly stretched his arms toward her enjoying the anticipation of the pleasure to come. He massaged her soft breasts. Excitement pulsed though him like electrical shocks.

Angelina's eyes blinked rapidly. "What?"

"Shhh, beloved. Shhh."

Her skin was silky and inviting. Ephraim stripped off her jacket and blouse then struggled with the twisted bra.

"No, no."

"Yes, yes," Ephraim whispered.

She rose from her unconscious state and lashed out with her arms, still fighting off Jud. "Stop it!"

"I cannot."

Ephraim pinned her arms down and gazed at both exposed breasts. He leaned down to suck on them.

Brenda's vision came into focus and she saw a grotesque Halloween mask descending upon her out of the shadows. She shrieked in horror, arched her back, and kicked up with her knees. Ephraim lost his balance and tumbled to the floor.

Trembling with fear and horror, Brenda tried to get off the mattress, but a strong hand reached from below the bed and grasped her right arm, trying to hold her down.

"No, No!"

Brenda looked along the arm to the bed edge and, in the moonlight, saw a malformed conical head coated with dried blood rise from the floor. She screamed till her breathe ran out. She tried to get off the bed, to get away from this monster, but the hold was strong. A short figure stood. Its other hand was stroking a large erect penis.

"Angelina!"

Brenda's heart raced. She could barely inhale at the sight of the revulsion before her. She franticly thrashed to get away, but the hand, the incredibly muscular hand, was pulling her toward the leaking penis. The shrieks continued in her head as she slid over the bed.

"Angelina, please!"

The words were as misshapen as the mouth that they came from. She finally managed to fill her lungs again and screamed, as if the sound would frighten her assailant. She held onto the mahogany carved headboard with her left hand kicking her feet at the grinning gargoyle.

Ephraim released his penis but held onto to her right arm. He went for her throat, replaying the first encounter.

His wet hand slipped. He quickly wiped it on the coverlet, ignoring her flaying right arm. With both hands now, he applied pressure.

Brenda struggled to rip the hold lose, but the strength was too much for her. She clutched the bed cover and labored to turn over. Her eyes enlarged and her face turned red. His monstrous features were close, and she could feel and smell his fetid breath.

Ephraim moved completely on top of her to keep Angelina from further kicking and rolling off the bed. She stretched to claw his face, but he leaned back. After a while, she was quiet—just like before.

Ephraim brushed hair from her eyes, caressed the vacant face, and then worked the ample breasts. He straddled her legs and entered. *It is so much better when she is warm.*

Clouds covered the moon and the bedroom became very dark. Only hard grunts and wet noises indicated that anything was alive in the room.

જ⁐જ

Monday began chilly and slightly damp. For the first time in a long while, Ash was anxious to get to school. The short bus ride to Grumm Road seemed long.

Along the okra-colored hall lockers, clusters of Wallkill Regional High School students talked excitedly under school spirit signs: *Go Rangers! WRV Rules, Eve-*

ryone is on the Team. Ash stopped near one group, pretending to adjust his backpack.

"Just disappeared."

"Nobody knows nothing."

"It's odd that both go at almost the same time."

Ash moved farther down the hall through activity that seemed different today. He heard snippets of animated conversation.

"What's going to happen to the football team?"

"He'll be back for sure."

"I don't know. Something's fishy here. This never happened before."

"They'll turn up. Where would they go?"

"Something's wrong."

Ash's interest increased. He sought someone on a lower social level to find out more, but a bell rang, indicating ten minutes to first class. Ash hurried to English III on the other side of the school.

In the brightly lit classroom, a beautiful specter sitting in the rear row glowed in black. Ash couldn't help but stare and his concentration led him to bump into a student in the first desk in row one.

"Watch it, fag!"

Not an auspicious entry. Everyone was laughing or smiling, except for the one in the back. Ash sat at his assigned seat, not daring to glance behind him, waiting for the lesson to be over. *This must be Luna.*

Finally, the class finished and the bell sounded. The

dash to the door began. Ash bucked the tide of students hurrying out and reached Luna as she packed her books.

"Hello, I—um—I'm Ash."

"I noticed you."

Her voice had a lilting sound that caressed Ash's ears. Her aroma of ripe berries, melons, flowers, and Arabian Sandalwood swirled around him, teasing his senses. She could be a female deity!

Ash couldn't stop surveying her. "Yeah, yeah, everyone did, I guess. I'm Ash."

"No, I mean I notice the way you are dressed."

"Oh, yes. You too."

Luna started for the door.

"What class do you have next?" he asked.

"American Studies."

"Who's the teacher?"

"Mr. Gordon, I think."

"Oh, okay. I'll show you where the class is."

"Thanks." She was pleased to have met another Goth and a cute one at that, despite the bruises, but she was used to seeing Alaric after being roughed up by uncaring souls.

Ash followed her out of the classroom, scolding himself for being so lame. He came alongside of her in the hall. "At the next intersection, we make a right. So you're new here." Another dumb question.

"Yes, today is my first day."

"Well, the classroom is the third door on the right.

So, I guess I'll see you at lunch." Not wanting to hear a negative reply and to be in time for his Algebra class, Ash rushed away.

After Algebra, Ash approached Freddy, a small tenth grade student, in the hall from behind. "What's up, Freddy?"

Startled, Freddy turned around. "Nothing," He was used to upper classman punching him on the arm, not speaking with him.

"What's all the talk about around here?"

"Oh that!" And he lit up with news. "Jud's gone!"

"Gone?"

"Yeah, and so is Brenda Armstead."

"What do you mean 'gone'?"

"Disappeared. Missing. Not here. Isn't that great?" Freddy broke into a big smile. Jud had shared bullying with everyone.

"Where did they go?"

"No one knows."

Ash had felt a lightness in the halls: students moving freely, without looking around, more laughter. This was why.

"Oh, and that's not all. It seems two others are also missing. They graduated last year."

"Four gone?"

"Yeah, and the rumor is that they were all sold into sex slavery! Someone is kidnapping young people here for sex. How exciting is that?"

The late bell rang.

"Thanks, Freddy," Ash hurried to his study hall, hoping to find Luna there, but was disappointed. He tried to concentrate on his assigned class work, but Luna and the news occupied his thoughts.

Lunch period finally arrived. Ash entered the food line, scanning for Luna. The cafeteria seemed extra slow. It was as if all seven hundred students were in line at the same time. Today's main menu consisted of chicken tenders with a pretzel rod or a hot roast beef bowl. Ash ordered a salad and vegetable soup. Holding the green plastic tray with both hands, he moved to the eating area and searched the tables. The room was almost filled. Chatter and food consumption permeated the hall with noisy emptiness. Ash couldn't spot Luna. Sitting at his usual place at a vacant table in the far end of the hall, he played with the salad and rehearsed what to say next time he saw her.

"Mind if I sit here?"

Ash looked up. Luna posed on the other side of the table.

"No, no. Sure. Have a seat."

She slid enchantingly onto the bench.

This was better than he expected. She actually sought him.

Both ignored the stares and whispers of those sitting at nearby tables.

"Are there any more Goths here?"

"I'm afraid not."

"How come just you?"

"Well, there are no free thinkers around here, and you'd think that being in the country would produce concern over the environment and how we are a part of it, but that's not true. Also conformity is the rule. I don't feel I belong here, you know what I mean?"

"Yes, I know the feeling—that's why I individuate."

"Yeah, I'm a distinct individual too, not one of the unthinking herd. It's often difficult."

"I know."

"Were there a lot of Goths where you came from?"

"Dover? No not many, just enough, though, that I didn't feel lonely."

"Are you Wiccan too?"

"Wiccan?"

"It's an ancient belief that all are equal. That no one is subservient to another. That the world is so complex, there can't be just one god, but many, and all are connected with our being, with nature."

"I've heard of it, but don't know much about it."

"There are rituals, but no set doctrines. It works better with a group, but there aren't any Wiccans out here. It helps me cope, you know?" Perhaps, Ash thought he went too far in this first conversation.

"Where did you learn about it?"

Ash blushed slightly. "The Internet."

"The Internet?"

"Yes, but I've read Silver Ravenwolf, Gerald Gardner, Raymond Buckland, and others," Ash added, trying to hide what might sound like naivety.

"Oh. My family is Lutheran. We're not involved in witchcraft."

"Some think Wicca is witchcraft, but it is so much more. I could teach you more about it. I mean, I don't want to convert you, but there is so much to learn. You'd really like it. You know the army recognizes Wicca and the *Handbook for Chaplains* gives guidance on Wicca religion. Wiccan groups have been given tax-exempt status and a US district court in Michigan recognized Wicca as a valid religion in 1988."

"I don't know. It's difficult being a Goth in Northern New Jersey already."

"How does your family feel about you being a Goth?"

"They tolerate it. My mother thinks it's a phase I'm going through. Dad was worried that I was hanging out with the wrong people. I think that's why we moved here, even though Dad claimed it was for his career."

"My parents are so concerned about me being a Goth—they have me seeing a psychologist. They don't know about Wicca."

"I don't know much either. I just don't know what the purpose of Wicca is."

Ash didn't want to chase her away with more religious talk. "Let me tell you about the school and about

Hamburg. Parts of it are actually interesting." Ash wondered if he was just babbling on.

Luna rose. "We'll see."

"How about this afternoon?"

"I've got a lot of unpacking to do."

"Oh, sure." Ash appeared dejected.

Luna realized she went too far in her coquettishness. If he was the only other Goth here, she didn't want to alienate him. "Well, okay."

"Great. Where do you live?"

"At 351 Falcon Ridge Way South."

"Wow, I live on Oak Street. Falcon Ridge South is almost in my backyard." Again, Ash felt slightly embarrassed over his enthusiasm.

Luna turned quickly so her hair flipped and her hips swayed. "See you later."

"All right! After school then." Ash immediately regretted bringing up Wicca so soon. He presumed in his innocence that Goth and Wicca went together. In truth, he knew little of Wicca. He should have asked more questions about her: what she liked, books she read. Damn! He followed the trim figure maneuvering gracefully between the lunch tables, remembered her scent and lavender eyes. He needed to do better the next time.

CHAPTER 10

Jay sat before Lieutenant Soldering on a late Monday afternoon.

"Rumors fly faster than creditable news. Take a look at the headline of this morning's newspaper." Soldering tossed a thin folded copy across the desk.

Hurray opened *The Advertiser News* and read the banner on the front page. "'Pied Piper of Hamburg!' What's this about?"

"It's about the missing couples: an assumption that someone is abducting our young people. Articles like this sell the paper."

"How did the paper find out?"

"From the parents, from the people you interviewed—it doesn't matter how. Gossip is all over the high school and throughout town. What matters now is that the story is out. Mayor Zicker is getting upset. What do you know so far?"

Jay opened the pad he'd brought in anticipation of this question.

"All were EMJs, residents of Hamburg, and attended WVR a year apart. The couples didn't know the other, had different friends, and didn't participate in any joint activities. Both boys have juvy records that are sealed."

"So we don't know shit."

"That's about it, Lieutenant."

"I talked with the mayor and we're asking for state trooper and FBI help."

"But the investigation is just under way. There are no immediate signs of foul play."

"Regardless of how or why they vanished, we need to get to the bottom of this. Mayor Zicker is quite concerned for the community, not to mention that elections are coming up. Four Hamburg youths are missing, Sergeant, four in a short period of time. I don't see a coincidence in this. And by calling in help, we can deflect any criticism on how we are handling it."

Jay failed to understand the significant of the newspaper. "You're saying I'm not competent?"

"No, I'm saying this is more than the department can handle and politics are part of it now. We need to solve this fast, before it gets out of hand. I want you and Hines to scour known teenage haunts like the castle and mill."

Jay grimaced. This was something he had planned on doing and forgot.

"I want you to interview acquaintances, students, and anyone who knows or recognizes these people. I want to be thorough for when the troopers and FBI come, and I want to calm the community. Appointments are being made to address civic and religious groups. The mayor will attend to the newspaper. I will talk to the high school today. We have to assure everyone there is nothing to fear, even though we know nothing."

☙☙☙

Ephraim awoke and quickly turned his head. Angelina was splayed out next to him. It wasn't all a dream. His small bit of happiness eroded as he caressed her thighs: cold already. Her large bright eyes, once bulging with surprise, were now cloudy and glassy, staring at something. Ephraim looked at the ceiling, hoping to find what fascinated her, and saw nothing.

All too soon, she too will have to go. Ephraim moved on top of her to take advantage of every minute left. She was rigid but satisfying.

Reluctantly, he washed, went to his room, dressed, and headed to the kitchen with Angelina's old clothes and his blood stained garments. His thoughts remained with the gratification he'd just shared. The balls of clothes he carried obscured his view as he tottered down. He didn't notice the boot on a step. Ephraim tripped on it and tumbled down the staircase to the floor below, landing face up. Dazed, he gazed above him. Large foggy cobwebs occupied the ceiling, wall corners, and edges. He turned his head, testing to determine if his neck was broken. The animals mounted over him at first seemed majestically indifferent to his fall. A silvery layer of dust, like early winter snow, covered their heads. Now, however, they seemed to come alive and captivated his attention for the first time in a long while. As he looked at each one, he sensed they wanted to tell him something: a secret or an answer. These wide blank eyes were holding something back. He stayed immobile, not wishing to disturb the moment, expecting an association. Maybe, maybe Uncle was trying to contact him. Ephraim looked up and focused on each mount, before he realized the eyes—the eyes were the key. In a birth of thought, he connected them with Angelina's eyes and realized a solution. He could keep her through the skills Uncle had taught!

ぐくぐ

Students filed nosily into the auditorium excited over missing their last class and buzzing over the reason for an all-school assembly.

On stage, the audio-visual crew set up a standing microphone and tested it.

"Hello. One, two, three."

The audience erupted in cat calls and jeers. Teachers tried to regain a nonexistent silence. The noise diminished slightly as Superintendent Bronner marched on stage, followed by the lieutenant. Bronner's gray three-piece suit was accented with a navy blue tie. The sharp pleats in his pants could cut raw meat. He stood straight, presenting what he knew would be an authoritative, masculine, figure.

"May I have your attention please!" Superintendent Bronner waited till clamor moderated enough to satisfy his authority. He stood tall, projecting an image he could only imagine.

A few dared to call out "Boner" before they were removed.

Bronner took off his wire-rimmed glasses for effect. "I want to address you today over the disappearance of two students and two former students. I know rumors have been flying around concerning this situation. Lieutenant Soldering is here today to fill us in on these events and the progress made so far. Lieutenant Soldering."

The students continued to whisper about sports, friends, activities—things that are more important than the antics of seniors and graduates.

Soldering stepped up to mic. "Good afternoon. I know there are a lot of gossip and stories going around today. I'm here today to reassure you that you have nothing to fear. There isn't—" The lieutenant needlessly made air quotes. "—a 'boogey man' abducting children, and there isn't a Chinese cartel selling adolescents into slavery. Don't believe hearsay and unfounded information and don't create any based on your guesses. True, we having missing people, but this doesn't necessarily mean harmful acts have been perpetrated. What I do want you to do is to be careful, as always. You need to be aware of your environment outside of school. Be observant of conditions and strangers. If you are planning to go somewhere, make sure someone knows where and for how long. Everyone should practice these things, regardless of the present situation. Your police force is on top of this. You have nothing to worry about or fear. I am quite sure the missing couples will show up. Thank you."

Soldering stepped back. Superintendent Bronner resumed command of the stage. He was silent as he gazed over his charges. The stage crew had focused a narrow-beam micro spotlight on his bald head creating a soft glow.

More students started to murmur and chatter, most withholding laughter. Bronner mistook this for concern and tried to ease it.

"Lieutenant Soldering is absolutely correct, in that there is no immediate danger to you. School schedules will proceed as usual. If, however, you feel anxious or apprehensive over this minor situation, my door is always open, as is that of our school counselors, Mr. Murray and Mrs. Joel. Your teachers are here for you, as well. Don't be afraid to express your feelings."

The ambient noise hadn't quieted down, despite the efforts of the teachers standing in the aisles.

Bronner didn't feel secure in the presentation so far but he continued toward ultimate failure.

"Any questions I can answer now?" he threw out as a life preserver.

Sensing the assembly could be over and time for class would remain, students looked at one another, hoping someone came up with a question. Those who had a reputation to maintain or wanted to create one took the challenge.

A senior stood and shouted, "What do you mean by Chinese sex trade?"

A teacher quickly made him sit down.

The superintendent ignored him and forged ahead to disaster. "Any other questions? Concerns?"

Teachers were staring at known troublemakers, sensing where this was going.

From somewhere in the middle row, a student said, "How will this affect the football team now that Jud is dead?"

Another, on a peer challenge, shouted out, "Is Noah involved—collecting two by two?"

Those who found the glowing bald spot comical now used the opportunity to release their pent up laughter.

Emboldened, more joined in. "I'd like to get out of this town too!"

"Check the motels!"

"I say good riddance to Jud."

"Hey—" Chad rose. "—who said that?"

"Your mother!" another anonymous voice retorted from somewhere in the auditorium.

Teachers were moving along the aisles and in the rows, trying to quell the outbreak. Ninth graders were giggling. Upper class students either saw amusement or took affront in the public verbal sparring.

Bronner finally understood that it was now over and waved his hand at the rows of students. "You are dismissed. You may return to class." He exited stage left as a collective moan arose at the quick close of the assembly.

The lieutenant was left center stage, watching the grumbling gathering file out, wondering if this had been worth the trouble or if it would cause trouble.

∽∾∽

"I'm going to help a friend with homework," Ash called to his mother as he shut the front door.

He used a shortcut through the woods in back to Luna's condominium. November was starting out cold. Tree limbs scratched the sky, looking for sunlight. On the way, he rehearsed his conversation. Breaths of condensed vapor carried his list away: *First comment on the assembly, then talk about Hamburg, ask about her, and if it seems right, bring up Wicca. Above all, don't be a jerk.*

Expecting to see Luna, he was surprised when Mrs. Brenson answered the door.

Looking at Ash, Charlotte immediately realized who the boy at the door must be. "Hello. You must be a friend of Heather's."

"I'm Korbin Miller."

"Well, do come in." She turned her head. "Heather—Luna, your friend is here."

An enchanting black manifestation moved smoothly into the room. Again, Ash was dumbstruck. "Hi."

Luna waited.

"Ah, um, what did you think of today's assembly?"

"Why don't you kids go into the study? I'll bring in some refreshments." Charlotte was happy to see that Heather had made a friend already. She was fearful that Heather's personality would prevent her from making friends in a new school setting.

Luna led the way to a first-floor bedroom converted to a den. She positioned herself on a tan couch, not behind the oak desk. Ash took notice and sat beside her, enhanced by her presence. She stood out in the neutral painted room. Ash tried not to stare.

"There were a lot of rude people," she said.

"What?" Her voice brought him back to reality.

"At the assembly, there were a lot of rude and unruly students."

"Oh, yes, yes there were."

"Did you know any of the missing?"

"Yeah, Jud and Brenda."

"What do you think happened?"

"I don't know—I don't care. Jud was a jerk."

"Did he push you around?"

Ash didn't want to admit to weakness. He looked down, trying to find the right thing to say.

Luna looked at Ash's face and, wanting to spare him, murmured, "He did. I knew his kind. It was the same in Dover High. We were always ridiculed and picked on."

Ash changed the topic, thankfully remembering the most important one. "Well, tell me about yourself."

Luna looked at Ash, deciding what to reveal. "Not much to tell. I lived in Dover since I was born. I like Bauhaus, The Sisters of Mercy, Blueberry, and A New Dawn. My favorite movies are *Dracula* with Bela Lugosi and *Suspiria*. My favorite author is Edgar Allen Poe and, of course, I watch *American Gothic*. I became a Goth when I met some Goths in middle school and we have been best friends since. There's a lot of pain in the world, not many want to face it, but it is part of being. You need to embrace all of life. My friends realized that. Sometimes I don't mind being apart, but I feel sad and alone sometimes. Being Goth helps with that. It helps me deal with it. That's about it. What about you?"

"I also like Bauhaus and The Sisters of Mercy. My favorite movies are *The Crow*, and *Pan's Labyrinth*. I watch *Sleepy Hallow*. My favorite author is H.P. Lovecraft. I became Goth because I wanted to feel like I belong somewhere, you know—not part of the unconscious mob." Ash looked into Luna's eyes and couldn't help what he said next, "We have a lot in common."

Embarrassed by this remark, he blundered onto another topic. "You know, Hamburg isn't such as bad place as this disappearance makes it out to be." He began to awkwardly recite: "There is skiing nearby and the Grand Cascades Lodge on Wild Turkey Way. It has a golf course, a tropical pool with a large water slide and a grotto-themed Jacuzzi, a bike park, and zip lines. There is a great view of the mountains from there. Then we have Ballyowen Golf Club and Owen's Pub on Wheatsworth Road, Cava Winery & Vineyard off Route 94—they have a great fig gorgonzola pizza." Ash stopped to take a breath.

"Any shopping malls?"

"There's one in Wantage about three miles away."

"Any movies theaters?"

"The nearest theater is in Sparta, nine miles away. And also nearby we have the Franklin Mineral Museum. It is the only spot in the world that has the mineral Franklinite, which glows red, blue, and green in a fluorescent light. And then there is the Wallkill River National Wildlife Refuge." Ash realized he was at the end of his list of attractions.

Luna appeared to be unimpressed. "That's it? No wonder they left town."

Ash didn't know how to continue.

Luna rescued him. "So what's this about Wicca? How did you get involved?"

Ash was happy and surprised by the return to the personal. "Well, its roots can be traced to the ancient agrarian Celtic society. Now it's a modern religion without the Celtic Halloween overtones. Wicca's a peaceful and balanced way of life. It sanctions oneness with all that exists. Nature was here first and we must respect it, enjoy its beauty, and give thanks to the creators. Wicca fosters free thought, the individual, and encourages an understanding of nature by affirming the divinity in all living things. Take a look around you. You may think you are in the sticks, but you are in harmony with nature. Religion is all around us, outside and inside. As I became a Goth, I became a Wiccan because of the need to be just me." Again, Ash paused. He wondered if he was rambling.

"Oh." Again, Luna seemed to be uninterested in Wicca. "We're Lutheran."

Ash pushed ahead. "That's okay." He wasn't really comfortable with Wiccan yet, but he was drawn to its principles. "We respect all religious work and the natural but invisible forces all around us. Wiccans have several basic beliefs: we revere nature, we use chants and creative visualization to focus psychic energy, we harm none, and we regard all living things as Sacred. A Wiccan may be considered a pagan, but there are tones of Christianity, Judaism, and Islam throughout it."

"What do you mean by 'we'?"

"Well, I don't have a coven, so I guess it's just me."

"How many form a coven?"

Ash perked up at this continued interest and maintained his monologue, trying to impress Luna. "More than one, but I do have a unique friend who might join." Ash hoped this last piece of information might increase her curiosity.

"Unique?"

એએએ

Jay pulled into the vacant, broken-tarmac lot across from the Gingerbread Castle entrance. Russet colored weeds eleven inches high were dying between the pavement cracks. Parking stripes were eating asphalt. No lines were whole, just large white spots that indicated where ones had been.

Corporal Hines felt his pants pocket for the search warrant, in case it might be needed, as he exited the car. He shivered as he left the warm interior.

Jay placed his officer's hat on his head and buttoned his jacket. A light breeze brought warning of cold times to come.

Dull low clouds were deciding whether to rain or snow and, with indecision, did nothing.

"Bring the flashlights," he ordered.

"It's daytime."

"Not in some of the dark places in there. Pad and pencil?"

Hines reached into the patrol car. "Yes. Do we need the camera?"

"No, I doubt we'll find anything definitive."

"What exactly are we looking for?"

"Anything that looks unusual or suspicious."

Hines looked across the road. "That could be a lot, could be little. Who knows? It's a mess over there."

"Well, let's go."

"Are we going to set up a zone or quadrant search?"

"No, just a walk through."

Jay opened a rusting lock with the key the current developers left with the department. The ornate flowered iron gate swung open to a chorus of eerie wails. Large grinding stones from the adjacent Wheatsworth Mill lined the unused entrance path. The cobblestone walkway complained as the men ground dirt and stones into its surface. Five decades of vacancy left more memories than structures. Seated on a ledge above, Humpty Dumpty didn't notice the intrusion and continued to contemplate his sad state.

"We'll start with the castle."

On the way up to the still-imposing building, the policemen quickly scanned the red dilapidated Old Lady Who Lived in a Shoe —nothing was noticeable.

Faded pink frosted turrets on the three-story rubble-stone castle still rose proudly into the melancholy November sky. Hugh stucco gum balls and cupcakes stubbornly clung on the exterior of the façade. Thick vines scaled the walls, struggling to get at the promised treats to suck non-existent nourishment. In front, a broken gate was all but hidden with old dying growth. It led to an arched doorway. Inside was the dark reproduction of a dungeon. Jay and Hines cast light on the debris scattered about the room. It was hard to tell if someone had been here recently, or if a struggle might have happened. A spiral staircase offered escape from the damp, decaying room to the main hall, which had contained figures—heroes and heroines from various fairy tales.

They had vanished like the era they were created in. In the middle of the floor was the round hole covered with a plum pudding grille opening to the basement. Triangular cut doorways opened to undersized alcoves where time worn wooden fairy tale figurines gazed up at the peeling paint and broken stained glass windows, waiting to be admired once more. No sign of life—no sign of human death on all floors.

Outside, Jay stopped and looked at the ground. Two long parallel tracks were slightly scraped into the earth. "What do you make of these?"

"Don't know. Could be kids dragging something."

"Hum, well, make a note of it. Seems fairly recent. We'll follow it on the way out."

The men moved past large broken and graffiti scrawled sculptures of Cinderella and Alice in Wonderland. Structural wires were visible through missing and deteriorated plaster. Someone had painted red hands on the breasts of both and punched sticks in the crutch. The officers traveled up the slope to the Old Witch's Cottage.

"Boy, this park has really gone to hell." Hines kicked a piece of rotting drywall. It disintegrated and left his polished boot caked with gypsum plaster. "Crap!"

"Watch your step. This place is a hazard waiting to happen."

"Why don't they just bulldoze it?"

"Expense, hazardous material, bureaucracy, regulations, historical value, you name it."

They arrived at the cottage.

"How we're going to get in? The wreckage and vines everywhere around this place won't allow us to get close. It seems all doors and windows are boarded anyway."

"Not this one window here." The sergeant pulled aside creepers and threw lose boards out of the way.

They scrambled through, entered, and surveyed the interior.

"Notice anything, Hines?"

"It's a mess and there's a cinder block in the middle of the floor."

"Anything else?"

Ned inspected the room. "No. Everything's in ruins."

"Look closer. There are chalk smudges around the block. Some parts of the room are dust free. And look at the shelves, there's candle wax."

"Yeah. And in the corner is a snack wrapper." Hines was proud that he observed something.

"Someone or some bodies were here. Make a note of this for FBI. Leave the wrapper where it is."

The two visited the old bakery, now smelling of mold instead of gingerbread; the defunct railway station; and the rest of the remains in the park and found nothing significant.

They then headed toward the two lines found earlier scratched in the ground.

"They seem to be leading toward the mill."

Following the shallow marks, they came to the chain-link fence and the cut opening.

"Well, we need to investigate the mill, anyway. Might as well enter here." Jay squeezed through followed by Hines, careful not to rip his leather coat. The scrapes led around the building to the gravel access lane on the side of the building side next to the river then ended.

Jay studied the disturbed dirt. "Looks like action here. I see footprints."

"Yeah. Probably some kids stuffing something in a car trunk they hauled away from the park."

"Well, make a note of it anyway, Hines. Don't step in the prints or tire marks. They're faint on this surface, but visible."

"There're a lot of them."

"Let the FBI sort it out. They're coming from Newark this afternoon and will stay at the Grand Cascades

Lodge. And state police from Troop in Augusta will assist with the investigations."

"Lucky them."

"But maybe not lucky for us. Channel Eight has picked up on the news. Bill Corning at the lodge says they reserved rooms too. They're bound to meet, but the Bureau will be quiet. I tell you, this is going to go big unless we find out where these kids are, so let's get this inspection over. We'll start at the front of the building and work back. Take the upstairs, Ned, but be careful of rotting stairs and floor boards. I'll meet you by the loading docks out back."

After an hour, the two finished the search.

"Find anything?" Jay asked.

"Signs of activity, but not recent."

"Me too. Let's head back. We'll take the access road."

Navigating crumbling cement steps, they came onto the loading area. Hines breathed in the crisp, clean autumn air. "I'm glad to get out of that place. Despite the chill, I like this time of year." He kicked a small pile of leaves and uncovered a charcoal scarf. "What's this?"

"Don't touch it." Jay bent down for a closer examination. "It's not wet or tramped down. Apparently it was recently dropped. Damn! This could be something. Ned, you had better go get the camera after all and bring a plastic bag. This could belong to one of the girls. And walk on the grass, not the roadway."

CHAPTER 11

At the head of the basement stairs, Ephraim turned on the switch for the cellar lights. Three weak ceiling bulbs only penetrated the immediate area below in a yellow haze. The outlying spaces of the granite block room remained dark, except in the far back area, where the big soot-stained Octopus coal furnace proudly glowed its red heart. Large asbestos and un-insulated ducts that let hot air rise and cool air in stretched into the ceiling. Field mice in the shadows halted their search for safe winter havens and spiders retreated to cracks and crevices at the intrusion. In the center of the cellar was a large, shiny, stainless steel table angled toward a hole in its corner wall. A sixteen liter galvanized bucket was directly under the hole with others stacked nearby. A high bay lighting fixture hung directly above the cold platform. Ephraim yanked on its string chain. Six fluorescence lamps blinked from a deep sleep then awoke. The table became bathed in white sterile light. This was Uncle's workshop. He was an expert taxidermist. Hunters would bring kills for him to mount this time of year. They came after Uncle's death, but Ephraim didn't open the gate for them and gradually they stopped coming.

A rough-hewn bench, built by Uncle for him, occupied the far side of the table. Memories were immediately triggered as he climbed upon it: the aroma of body effluvia and Lysol disinfectant, the gentle red and yellow glistening flow of internal fluids, and the sound of it pouring, then dipping into the bucket below. This was where he had felt the closest to Uncle. This was as near to a family activity as he ever had. This was where Uncle taught. Ephraim looked across the dissection table and could see him about to slice open a buck.

"The dead are not meant to be hidden, Ephraim, but to be admired forever. The ancients knew this. But what do we do? Embalm then hide. Did you know, Ephraim, the British philosopher Jeremy Bentham made other plans for his body after death in 1832? He now sits proudly in a wooden cabinet in the main building of University College in London. True, he is just a skeleton wearing clothes filled with hay, but Bentham's head was mummified. He was a visionary. They did not have the techniques then as we do now. The Egyptians were on the right track, but some cultures have actually have been successful in preserving entire bodies without wrappings, without mummification as chemical technologies improved." He raised his knife to make his point." In fact, dear boy, Vladimir Lenin, Eva Perón, little Rosalia Lombardo, St. Bernadette, Ho Chi Minh, and others were remarkable preserved. Eva Perón so much that a caretaker was driven mad by sexual fantasies about her. Imagine that!"

Carefully pinching the deer, he nicked the skin at the genitals and inserted the blade under the skin neatly slicing the length of the body to the rib cage. "Taxidermy is a much better preservation, and while this means is acceptable for animals, most of society has not yet realized the advantage for humans. Embalming merely reserves a hunk of meat and then after all the treatment, a stone to memorialize the departed. Taxidermy is not only an art, Ephraim, it is a God-given way to celebrate life. Why just have a grave for a boring horizontal loved one? Taxidermy can create the person as he or she was most remembered: sitting at a desk, standing in a kitchen, playing badminton—endless possibilities. Some may think I am just a buffer, lad, but, and I do not want to crack up, give me a sound croaker, and I know I could create a true lifelike person, indeed, a lasting companion as best recalled. Death does not have to take everything to the crematorium or the ground. And it shouldn't be disguised as sleep." Uncle reached in, cut the deer's windpipe and rolled the internal organs onto the table.

Ephraim turned toward the back wall. Outside Uncle and Angelina were deep in the cold damp ground. No burn scars or wounds had damaged them—it was a tragic mistake he had made and only now recognized and regretted. He was a josser, a juggins! How stupid was he! Living apart probably slowed thought processes. Ephraim repeatedly slapped his head in remorse. He was a stupid, stupid person. This, though, this would be a new beginning. He certainly would not be alone anymore.

Ephraim hopped off the bench and checked the dust covered Edwardian beech cabinet standing against the wall opposite the table. He turned each key for each of the six drawers and pulled the doors down. The supplies were where Uncle had last put them. Ephraim lovingly ran his thumb along the blades of the old skinning and fleshing knives in the top right section—the edges were still sharp. In the drawer below were sewing needles, gut thread, and string. The bottom compartment contained a large box of non-iodized salt, plastic bags, and a reddish-brown-stained cloth apron. In the top left drawer was a marvelous tray of glass eyes, paint, and makeup. Borax and alcohol occupied the middle left section. The borax was lumpy, but would suffice, and the alcohol had remained strong. The salt was hardened, but more was in the kitchen. From the right bottom, he removed a box of surgical gloves, not entirely pliable, but serviceable. All the items necessary were available. He placed them reverently on the work bench near the table then dragged the stand from the other side for easy material retrieval while at work. Ephraim checked the white plastic utility sink opposite the table. It was relatively clean and the hose attached to its faucet was still viable. Next to it was a Victrola covered with a satin sheet. Ephraim removed the cloth. The "Pachelbel Cannon in D" record was on the turntable where Uncle had left it. Ephraim gently touched the record player. It had soothed him many times. Finally, he positioned an ebony canvas trunk containing excelsior and yellowing newspaper close by.

He stepped away to admire and remember the set up. Everything was perfect—warm memories again flowed through him.

In the kitchen, salad and soup bowls were measured by the spread of Ephraim's hand. The correct fit was necessary. He found a storage container he judged to be the right size. The pantry contained two boxes of gelatin. Over ten minute periods, Ephraim mixed the contents into a large bowl of warm water. When the consistency was right, he poured the mixture into the two soup bowls and the container he had greased with butter and put them in the avocado GE refrigerator to cool. It would be ready for the final process.

He was now prepared to proceed.

Angelina stared at the ceiling with shrunken eyes, unaware of her immortality to come.

ᙩᙄᙩ

"Knock, knock." Charlotte entered with glasses of cider and a plate of chocolate chip cookies.

"Oh, thanks, Mom, just put the tray down anywhere."

Smiling, Charlotte placed the tray on the desk, rearranged the glasses and plates, and backed out of the room, smiling.

"So who is this unique friend?" Luna asked.

"Actually, I just met him. He lives out by High Point."

"High Point?"

"It's a state park and the highest point in New Jersey. The Appalachian Trail runs through it. The Cedar Swamp in it is the farthest inland swamp in the country containing white cedar trees. It's nature at her best, even though it's a very lonely place."

"You met this guy there?"

"Yeah, I was taking a walk, you know, enjoying the beauty, and met him along the way. He's a special person. He lives by himself in an old mansion set far into the woods next to the swamp."

"Wow. Is this why he's so special?"

"Sure, that, and I think he's a dwarf, and he speaks funny—may be because his face is deformed and he uses words I really don't understand."

"What?" Luna made a face, indicating disbelief.

"Okay, okay, let me get this straight. From what you have just told me, I'm in a town with a fairy tale castle and an ugly dwarf living in the woods. When does Snow White appear?"

"It's the truth, believe me."

"Sure, and oh, yes, there's a Pied Piper luring children out of town too!"

"They're not children and that has nothing to do with what I just told you."

"Well, you've had your fun and I thank you for coming over." Luna started to stand.

"No, no I'm not joking with you—I'm serious. Ephraim is his name and he's very real. He's lonely and needs friends. Please sit down. I thought you would understand." Ash held his hands in front, palms toward Luna and lowered them in the air as if he had a Wiccan force to use. "Please sit down."

Luna glared at Ash but decided to listen. She sat a little farther away, though.

"Thank you. Thank you. Ephraim has an inherited condition that made him small and fat. His face is scarred—I don't know how, but all these things made people fearful of him, and he's afraid to go out 'cause people would probably ridicule him and run away, or worse. But he's really a nice innocent guy who just needs friends."

"And this is the one you want to create a coven with?"

"Yes, but it's not as lame as it seems."

"Really?"

"Yes, really. I know what it's to be an outsider and so do you. You can't judge people by their looks. You ought you know that!"

"True."

"He needs friends. It's not so much about a coven as it's about befriending him, and we can be his friends. He's all alone. I mean, he doesn't have a television or radio. I don't know if he even knows they exist."

"What does he do all day?"

"I don't really know that either. He said he's read all of Mr. Dickens's novels more than once and others like Jane Austen and some guy named Ainsworth."

"He sounds creepy."

"Maybe, but he is so alone. He needs people around him. He needs our help!"

"Our help? I don't know about that."

"You don't know about me either, but we can become friends."

Luna sat still, without expression. She finally took a sip of the cider. Ash didn't know if this was a rejection of him, Ephraim, or both. He took a cookie for something to do. Luna looked directly at him, into his eyes, as if she was searching for his soul.

Ash replaced the uneaten cookie and leaned forward for one more attempt. "Look, I don't really know you either, Luna, but I can tell you have compassion. I'm willing to give friendship with you a try and I'm willing to be friends with Ephraim. It doesn't cost anything, except a little effort and a willingness to risk disappointment. Shouldn't you be willing to reach out to show the kindness others have refused to give to you?"

"This is strange."

"I'll admit that it is, but you have to follow your heart. What does your heart say? It is the truest guide in life. And I sense you have a good heart. You know? I took up Wicca to find a better way without knowing what was right at my doorstep. I was selfish and—and I relished in that. Then I found a soul in need of companionship: Ephraim. And now I found you! If I'm true to myself, I can't let these opportunities pass. But even if you don't want to be a friend to Ephraim, I hope you will be my friend."

"Do you drive?"

"Yes, when I can borrow my mom's car."

"You want me to go to a remote park with someone I just met to meet an ugly dwarf!"

"You make it sound creepy and I'm not just someone!"

"It is creepy. Why doesn't he meet you somewhere—like the castle?"

"He's only left the house once."

"So he has a car and never leaves the house?"

"The car was his parents' and I told you he doesn't want to be seen by people."

"Yet, he wants you for a friend and perhaps others."

"Yes, I'm his friend now. Probably the first friend he's ever had. He's starting to live. He really doesn't want to continue as a hermit."

"How old is this guy?"

"I don't know. It's hard to tell."

"He's ugly?"

"He's different. What is 'ugly' anyway?"

"I don't know. But I'm new here—I need time to get used to things. This is so bizarre. I just don't know."

"Okay, I think I understand. It was enjoyable talking with you, anyway. Maybe we'll see each other in school again." Ash rose, rubbing his thighs, not wanting to leave.

Luna concentrated on the juice and cookie platter.

Ash turned toward the door and half waved. "Goodbye."

"Oh—"

Ash faced Luna at this uttering, hoping.

"Maybe we can talk about it more."

Ash wanted to express joy and relief. Instead, he sat down with a big smile.

"Ash, if this guy lives in the woods, how would we see him?"

"I could borrow the car and we could ride up."

"Do you know he really wants to see you again?"

"Yes, he really wants friends."

"Do your parents know about him?"

"My parents are already concerned about the beating I took. I don't need to have them fret over anything else."

Luna slowly shook her head. "So you do think there may be a problem?"

"No, no, I didn't mean 'fret' in that way. They just never understand me."

"This too much to take in. This just doesn't sound right."

"But he's a nice person. Nothing would happen, I promise you that. I could ask my mother for the car on a weekend. I'll tell her I want to take my new friend hiking. She'd jump at that. Would your mother allow you to go out?"

"I guess so—she's happy too that I've made a friend."

"Even in the short time I met him, Ephraim seems like a decent person, you know? Just so lonely. So what do you think?"

"I'm still nervous about meeting some deformed dwarf in the woods."

"It'll be all right, I assure you. I'll be there. Really, you have nothing to worry about."

"What would we do?"

"Just talk with him. Let him know about the outside world. I'm anxious to find out what he does all day. Can you image being alone for a long time? He needs some companionship. This is a chance, Luna, a chance to really help someone."

Luna again considered the suggestion. It would be exciting and she knew the deep hurt of ostracization. She looked Ash directly in the eyes. She felt she could trust him. "All right, as long as we make it a short visit."

"Great! Sure, a max of two hours, and maybe we can even take a short hike afterward. I've lived here all my life and never have seen the Cedar Swamp."

"Well, I don't know about the swamp. When do you want to go?"

"How about this Saturday?"

"Is this Ephraim really ugly?"

"Outwardly he's scarred, but inside he's a very nice guy. You can take it. I'm sure you've seen ugly in people before."

Luna took a deep breath. This was so much on her first day, but she didn't want to isolate herself like Ephraim. No one except Ash had approached her in school. "All right, all right."

ↃↄↃↄ

"Sergeant Jay Hurray, this is Special Agent James Davy." Lieutenant Soldering introduced the two men. "The sergeant was first on the case, Special Agent Davy. Jay, we asked the Bureau to become involved since these two incidents could be kidnappings, serial killings, or involuntary servitude, or slavery."

"Really? Involuntary servitude or slavery? This is just the ridiculous rumor floating around now."

"We have to process all avenues, Sergeant."

"The lieutenant is correct in that aspect. The sooner we become involved, the faster this can be solved. We sent hair samples found on the scarf and expect preliminary results in a few days. In the meanwhile, I'd like to visit the parents' houses for a visual identification. I've ask the lieutenant to cordon off the mill area. State troopers are on alert, in case we need manpower to properly search the area."

Jay sighed. "Hines is out there now."

"All right, let's get this over with. I'll drive." Special Agent Davy was through the door before Jay could stand.

Maria Portny answered the door wearing the same lime green terry cloth bathrobe she had on during the first visit.

Between her fingers was the cigarillo. "News? You've brought news about Dawn? Is it good news? "

"Mrs. Portny, do you recognize this?"

Special Agent Davy produced the plastic bag.

Maria grabbed it and studied the scarf, kneading the fabric through the plastic with her fingers. "No, no, I don't."

"This doesn't belong to your daughter?"

"No, no. Not that I'm aware of. It seems very expensive."

"Are you sure?"

Maria handed the bag to the sergeant. "Yes, I'm sure. What is this all about?"

"We found it and thought it might be linked to your daughter's disappearance." Jay passed the scarf to Special Agent Davy. "Thank you for your time."

"Wait!"

"You haven't heard from Dawn then." Davy's tone was a statement rather than a question.

"No, I haven't. Is there anything else? Do you have any idea where she might be? I'm beginning to worry now."

"We're doing the best we can. Special Agent Davy is with the FBI to help us solve this."

"FBI? Are terrorist involved? Why the FBI?"

"They have the experience in missing cases. We want to solve this as quickly as possible. I'll keep you informed of our progress, Mrs. Portny."

Jay brought his hand to his visor, Davy nodded, and they left Maria standing in the doorway.

"I didn't think it was Dawn's and I only hope it's not Brenda Armstead's, Special Agent Davy."

"If it isn't, we are at a dead end." Davy realized it was a poor choice of words.

June nearly fainted as she recognized the scarf. Jay helped her to the sofa.

"I—I gave this to her for her birthday. She would never lose it. Where did you find it?"

"We are going to search thoroughly for her, Mrs. Armstead," Davy assured her.

"Search? Is she lost? I know she's alive. I feel it. Where did you find the scarf?"

"We don't know if she is lost, ma'am. We will find out."

"Is, is she hurt?" June started to cry. "Where is she?"

"We don't know yet if she's hurt. Is there a neighbor we can contact to be with you?"

June removed one hand from her wet eyes and pointed right. "April Marky."

"It's okay, the sergeant will get your neighbor and call headquarters to get in touch with your husband."

After Mrs. Marky took control of June, Jay and Davy headed to police headquarters. Special Agent Davy resumed command. "Now we a have beginning. We need a plan. Sergeant, I need you to contact the town's voluntary firefighters. I'll get the lieutenant to call in all off-duty officers. We're going to need all the manpower we can get. Call the medical examiner. Notify Hines that he is officially at a crime scene investigation. He's to keep outside the castle and mill areas and not let anyone in. We need to have a guard scheduled until the morning. Do you still have viable search warrants for the castle and mill?"

"Yes, and we can also call in Grange members."

"All right, have everyone meet at headquarters tomorrow at seven. We have to act quickly to secure the search area."

∽∾∽

James Davy showed up at six. Eleven men were already waiting.

Lieutenant Soldering took Davy aside. "You're in charge here. You have the experience, we don't."

The agent just nodded.

"Mr. Armstead has been calling since last night."

"What was he told?"

"Only that we found the scarf. He demanded to know where it was found. The desk officer told him nothing."

"Good, we don't want him contaminating the area."

The break room had been converted to a command post. A five-foot tan folding table was placed in the middle of the room. Pads, pens, and large paper sheets covered the top. On a side shelf, the Keurig had been pushed aside for a twelve-cup coffee maker brought over from the Grange.

"I want to thank all of you for coming." Davy drew a rough sketch of the castle and mill and outlined the vicinity around them with a thin line marker. In the corner, he wrote the location, date, time, and his name, leaving room for weather and lighting conditions at the scene. "This is the area we need to search. Before going in, Corporal Hines has photographed the outside grounds starting with the mill. The inside was preliminarily searched, so we will save that for a thorough examination later. Scrape marks were found leading from the castle to the mill access road and, since the scarf was found near the end of the marks, we will start there, using an outward spiral pattern. The castle and park will be the secondary search." Davy drew a clockwise coil with its center on the dirt road by the loading docks. "Everyone take a pad and pen. Record anything out of place: broken twigs, disturbed leaves, anything that seems out of the ordinary. Search under debris or fallen logs—anyplace something may be hidden. If you come across possible evidence, such as blood traces, pieces of clothing, jewelry, or foot prints, yell out and don't move farther. Write in detail what you see. Remember, this could be a possible murder scene. Please be thorough, slow, and quiet. Trooper Brown—" Davy nodded to the blue uniform behind him. "—will be handling any evidence we find. Any questions, gentlemen?"

All remained silent, thinking about this depressing undertaking.

"Finish your coffee. Do not bring the cup with you. The ladies' auxiliary will have beverages and food available in the parking lot, well away from the investigation. Do not smoke, chew gum, or leave anything behind in your search. Sergeant, make sure we bring plastic bags, latex gloves, a shovel, and a broom handle or something like it."

The group loaded into cars and pickups and headed to the mill. Gray clouds were not uniform and gave hope that sunlight would break through. A number of black crows perched on barren tree limbs hoarsely cawed, giving warnings to what might be ahead for the gathering men in the parking lot across the street.

Lieutenant Soldering stood with Special Agent Davy as he addressed the men before they proceeded to the designated search area. "I want all of you to be methodical. Don't overlook anything. The scarf was found in a pile of leaves so things may not always be visible. There is no rush here. The sergeant gave you your line positions. We will form a tight position, four together, behind another four, elbow-to-elbow and spiral out. When you reach the building, continue past it back into the circle. Just because someone has walked it before you doesn't mean the area is clean—he may have missed something. When we have finished the first search, we will begin again at another location. Okay, gentlemen, let's proceed to the beginning of the mill access road."

At the road entrance, Soldering introduced Special Agent Davy to Doctor Brenson. "The Doctor is our new certified medical examiner."

"I hope we won't need you," Davy said. "Sergeant, is it clear to walk on the access road?"

"Yes, I just completed photographing the length of it and we made plaster casts of discernible tire marks. There were no clear shoe marks and the road up to the scarf location was thoroughly searched."

"Corporal Hines."

Hines stepped from the group.

"Are you finished photographing the loading docks and the scarf location?"

"Yes, sir."

"Good. Let's proceed."

Before the searchers entered the road, a white Toyota passing by on Gingerbread Castle Road came to a sudden halt and the driver, Paul Armstead, raced to the assemblage and pushed to the head of the group. "Is this it? Is this were the scarf was found? My god, so close to home! Is Brenda there? Did you find my daughter?"

Special Agent Davy stepped in front of Paul. "Mr. Armstead, calm down."

"Calm down? Calm down? Is my daughter there? Is she alive?"

"We don't know."

"You don't know? What are you doing here?"

"We are just searching areas of interest."

"With this many men, I don't think so. Do you know of anything about Brenda?"

"Look, I'll be honest with you—this is where the scarf was found. We don't know more than that."

"What? She could be in there? I'm going in."

"No, no, you're not. We need to be thorough and document everything. I'll personally let you know what we find, all right?"

"No, no, no. You didn't tell us the scarf was found here. I don't trust you. She's there, isn't she?"

"You have to let professionals handle this. Please

leave. We may find nothing more than the scarf. It doesn't necessarily mean she is still there. There's nothing you can do here. I'll let you know our findings, I promise."

"But you think she might be there. That, that she might be dead." Paul made an attempt to get past Davy, but the lieutenant and sergeant were now blocking the way as well. "Look, look, if it's my daughter, I have the right to know!"

"Mr. Armstead, I can't let you in on an official investigation. We don't know if your daughter is involved and that is the truth."

"Official investigation, well I'm her father! How official is that?"

"Please calm down."

"Don't patronize me." Paul continued to struggle past the men. "What are you hiding?"

"Nothing Mr. Armstead, nothing at all." Jay stared directly in Paul's eyes, willing him to retire.

After a futile more attempts, Paul finally accepted the situation. He felt weak and frightened. "All right, okay, I'll expect you'll notify me as soon as you learn something."

"Certainly."

"As soon as you learn something, you hear that?" Armstead returned to his car, composed himself, and slowly drove away.

Jay watched him drive away and said, more to himself than anyone, "I thought he was in control when I interviewed him. He snapped pretty fast. I hope he doesn't do anything stupid."

"You never know what humans are capable of, Sergeant. All right, men let's get this over with." Davy led the group up the road.

With attention on what lay ahead, no one noticed that the white car had returned and pulled into the parking lot across the road to the right of the van where the auxiliary ladies were focused on making coffee and preparing rows of donuts on a card table. The driver of the car sat and stared intently toward the mill road.

At the dock lot, Jay arranged the men. When all were lined up, he signaled to begin by raising and lowering his right arm. The dry leaves crackled as the men circled off the road and onto the river bank. The air was clear and crisp—no odors of putrefying flesh.

The men started to relax. So far, it was a lovely walk in the woods.

"Wait!" a granger shouted.

The entire party came to a halt.

"What is it?" Davy called out.

"Some disturbance in the leaves. Seems like two flattened lines leading downhill."

"Please note what you see. Hines, go take photos. Be careful where you step. Everyone remain where you are."

Davy moved next to the man, who pointed out the slight impressions. Though barely visible, they ended at the river edge. He patted the man's shoulder. "Good eye!"

With Hines in front digitally documenting the traces, Special Agent Davy carefully arrived at the river's edge. "Take photos of the tracks uphill. Someone pass the broom handle down here."

The muddy Wallkill River flowed slow and thick. It pooled into the dam before escaping through cracks and broken concrete. A light morning mist swirled on the lazy current, which produced a languid eddy pirouetting a few feet in front of Davy. He could see something near the surface causing a backwash as the river flowed over it. The agent poked the broom pole into the eddy then extended his hold farther up the handle to reach nearer the circular motion and dipped in again. The wooden tip hit something. "Something's there, maybe a rock. I need a volunteer."

A firefighter raised his hand. "Here!"

"Okay, swing way around to avoid the tracks and walk along the river edge to me. Go slow and look at the ground as you go for anything not natural."

When the firefighter arrived at Davy's side, the agent handed him the pole. "Wade out to where the eddy is. See it there?" A head nod. "Use the handle or if the object is close enough to the surface, your hand, and find out if it's a rock, old machinery, or anything else."

The volunteer removed his jacket and went nearly waist deep into the cold water to reach the eddy. All watched as he tapped the stick along what appeared to be a large object. He immersed his arm into the pool, his head inches above the water and traversed the object.

Special Agent Davy knew what he discovered from the man's face. "Call for a tow truck."

The search party was ushered across the street, gathered around the van, and consumed the coffee and donuts. Low whispers carried questions and perceived answers. The gray November morning matched the mood of the gathering.

Bill Harper arrived in fifteen minutes with his International medium-duty wrecker.

The chilly firefighter reluctantly dropped the blanket he had been given, went back into the water, and hooked the towing cable to what he thought was a front bumper. The rest of the car was steeply angled.

Harper engaged the winch clutch and a midnight blue '65 Ford Galaxie, leaking brown water, was slowly hauled up the embankment onto the road.

"That looks like Jud Robinson's car," Jay whispered to Davy.

Davy opened the driver's side door. A bloated white body with green discoloration was sprawled on the front bench seat.

"Doctor!"

Brenson was already heading toward the leaking Ford. He snapped gloves on and bent into the car. He turned the body to view the face. There wasn't one.

"Is it recognizable, Doc?"

"No, no, I'm afraid not—the face has been beaten to a pulp. The facial bones have been pulverized. I think we can assume that was the cause of death, not drowning, till a proper autopsy. There aren't any indications of a long immersion—severe wrinkling of the skin of the palms, loosening of general skin, hair, or fingernails. Judging from the haircut and clothes, it appears to be male. Apart from that, there is nothing more I can determine now."

"When did he die?"

"Rigor Mortis starts to wear off after about thirty-six hours. However, rigor mortis can be altered by the water current and temperature. Unless someone witnessed the body entering the river, there is no reliable method for determining the length of time that it has been submerged. At the autopsy, we have other means of dictating time of death such as food in the stomach. A light meal vacates the stomach within one and a half to two hours, a medium meal is out of the stomach within three to four hours, and a heavy meal is eliminated within four to six hours."

"Can you tell if he died here or somewhere else?"

"Livor mortis or discoloration shows in the parts of a body not making contact with an object. So a body lying on its back will show lividity in the small of its back, its neck etc., but not in the body parts directly touching a hard surface. Again this has to wait till autopsy since I won't remove clothes here."

Special Agent Davy turned toward Lieutenant Soldering. "Well, it appears we have a murder here."

"Seems so."

"After the ambulance leaves, get the men back and let's finish the land and building search. Trooper Brown, please notify the State Police Marine Services Bureau in Lake Hopatcong. We have to search the dam and the waters below. If that is Robinson, the girl might be nearby."

The driver of the white Toyota became rigid as the tow truck arrived. He gripped the steering wheel, in certainty of what was found when the ambulance appeared, and held it white-knuckle tight till it left, followed by Bill Harper with a blue Ford in tow. Paul recognized the car as Jud's. Indecision lasted only a moment. Paul followed the ambulance. He needed to see what was in it and then go to Harper's. He probably could get more information from Bill.

CHAPTER 12

As before, Ephraim folded Angelina in the bed sheets and carefully slid her off the bed. Gripping the cloth by her head, he slowly dragged her down the stairway to the basement door. The steep cellar steps weren't carpeted. Ephraim didn't want to bruise her further, so he lowered Angela's head and thought. The carcasses of the deer and bears that Uncle worked on were either passed through a basement window or were hauled down by the hunters. He couldn't do this with Angelina for fear of dropping her. Ephraim sat and thought some more. Thinking was difficult, but Uncle was truly guiding him as he gazed at the hallway carpet. Moving Angelina aside, he struggled to pull the long Persian runner toward the stairs and then down to the bottom. All the rough wooden steps were now covered, establishing a suitable path to the cellar.

Uncle used a pulley system to hoist his work onto the table. Again, Ephraim was fearful of bruising the now grayish-white stretched skin with the coarse ropes. He positioned her on the bench, sitting up, and rested beside her.

He rubbed her arm, comforting her. "I will take care of you, love. You will not want to leave again."

Ephraim stood, removed the sheet, and, with a concentration he hadn't experienced in a while, took a hold of the body under the arms, and lifted the upper half onto the table. Cradling the legs, he placed them on the cold surface. This had to be done right. There would be no second opportunity.

Bright lights revealed Angelina's condition that had been hidden by the dark bedroom: blue fingers and toes, a tinge of green throughout the waxy ashen body, opaque eyes, and mouth partially open from a swollen tongue. Ephraim didn't see or smell these states or the leaking odor of putrefaction as he admired his prized beauty.

He pushed her farther from the table's edge. He needed to turn her on her stomach. Skinning would be more difficult working from the back, but he didn't want stitch marks on the good side. He rolled her over then pulled her nearer to the edge. He was almost ready.

Ephraim wound the Victrola and placed the needle on the record. The melodic progression of three violins, a piano, and cello filled the room and reverberated through the stone wall cellar, filling all the dark places. Uncle claimed Pachelbel's eight bars of music repeated twenty-eight times relaxed him and brought forth his best artistic talents, giving grace to his creations. Ephraim found the same solace in all music and often came down to play the Victrola, especially in times of depression and loneliness.

Ephraim splayed Angelina's legs and separated the buttocks to expose the anus. Her derriere was smooth and still firm, though discolored. Ephraim caressed each side and became hard. This enticing view was new. He dropped his pants and climbed back on the table between her legs. Grabbing her waist, he pushed her thighs apart with his knees till her posterior was vertical, and, after a bit of fumbling, entered. The exhilaration flowed from his penis throughout his entire body and increased with each thrust.

Spent, Ephraim stood again on the stand. After thanking Angelina, he dressed, pulled on the surgical gloves with some difficulty—he had to stretch his fused right fingers into one area. He selected a skinning knife, the one he knew to be Uncle's favorite. With his left hand, he positioned the knife tip in her wet anus and, with a sigh, proceeded to cut upward between each buttock. At the base of her spine, he pinched the skin and worked the knife evenly along the inside to loosen it, peeling it back with his other hand. The gasses trapped inside the stretched skin made the peeling easier as they escaped.

The odor was so strong that it finally registered with Ephraim, but he continued to cut till he reached the neck then stepped down and back. He wiped his sweating brow with his shirt sleeve. An exhaust fan would have been nice. He took a piece of cloth and wrapped it over his nose.

Flaying her head would be a problem. For now, Ephraim improvised as he continued on the body. He sliced and pealed each arm. After a moment's thought, he took a cleaver and chopped off both hands at wrist. It would be too difficult to treat each blue finger. Returning to the lower part, Ephraim began to remove the feet and the bothersome toes. The cleaver was inefficient at cutting through the tibia and fibula. A hacksaw finished the work. Ephraim removed the feet at the ankle joints, cracking them off like a chicken leg from a thigh. All these pieces were thrown in the metal bucket below the table just as the third violin entered with the follower melody.

Ephraim took a deep breath, inhaling the sweetness of the music, rolled his shoulders to relieve tension, and continued with the work before him.

He incised around the neck and continued to peal. He rolled Angelina over and ever so cautiously scraped thin skin from muscle and fat, taking extra care with the breasts and groin.

After almost nine hours of work, Ephraim had a cadaver showing white tendons, pink muscles and a pile of loose graying skin. He stuffed the skin in a bucket of cool water with a small capful of Lysol and table salt. This would soak overnight.

Ephraim moved to the head. Slicing up the back, he peeled the scalp and, ever so carefully, the skin around the face. He placed this entire piece in another bucket of cold mixture.

The oils in a brain provided a natural tanning solution. Using a hacksaw, Ephraim removed the skull cap and scooped out the organ. He took the brain to the kitchen and cooked it on the wood burning stove in an iron pot with a cup of water till it broke down and resembled porridge.

Ephraim placed the solutions in the refrigerator and checked on the gel. Everything was going fine. He glanced looked outside—it was early morning and that made him realize how tired he was. He didn't feel hungry, but looked back in the refrigerator for some snack. Nothing appealed to him. He decided to rest before continuing and wearily, but happily, went to his room and climbed on the bed for much-needed sleep.

෧෨෧෨

Paul tried not to think as he followed the ambulance. Right now there wasn't bad news, not yet, not till he discovered what was inside. Right now everything was all right. But thoughts stabbed at his conscience: the strobe lights and siren weren't on—there didn't seem to be a rush to the hospital. This could mean only one thing: this wasn't a life or death situation, probably just death.

The driver and EMTs casually exited in front of Saint Clare's emergency entrance. Paul parked in behind a television van and ran toward the rear doors of the van. He stopped, afraid to get closer. Fearful of what he might come to know.

The EMTS appeared and ignored him, laughing at a private joke. One pulled the door open—the other stepped on the bumper and grabbed the gurney. Both rolled it out. The wheels dropped with a sudden metallic screech. Paul flinched. On the gurney was a zipped black body bag. Nothing alive could be inside the ominous carrier.

"Who is that?" Paul asked.

"Dunno some kid."

"A kid?"

"Yeah, some teenager."

"Who?"

"Dunno that either. His face was bashed in beyond recognition."

His. Paul relaxed. It was a male. It wasn't his daughter. His relief was short lived as he realized he still didn't know where his daughter was. "What happened?"

The EMT just shrugged his shoulders.

A reporter rushed out of the emergency room, signaling his camera man to follow him. Paul quickly returned

to his car. On his way to Harper's, Paul noticed the television broadcasting vans heading in the direction of the
mill. Somehow, the search and result had been leaked to
the press. All the stations were represented: ABC, CBS,
Fox, NBC, WNET, and Spanish Telemundo and Unimas.
The "Pied Piper of Hamburg" had caught the interest, not
only of New Jersey, but of the country.

One bay was closed. Paul found Bill Harper in the
other under the engine of a Volvo. He didn't provide any
information. Though, Randy Mcgreen did volunteer that
the Ford was Jud's before Bill gave him a stern look and
Randy pretended to work on the brakes of the S60 T6 on
the lift.

Paul sat in his car, frustrated by the lack of information gained, thankful that Brenda was not a part of the
little he did get, and afraid of what this actually meant.
Not wanting to go to work, needing to do something, Paul
drove back to the mill.

The vans were parked along Gingerbread Castle
Road, satellite dishes pointed east. Camera operators and
reporters crowed around the mill access road, interviewing anyone who breathed. Paul slowly drove past and
turned into Bluffs Court, stopping two blocks from the
house so June wouldn't see the car. He removed his car
coat and tan suit jacket and placed them, neatly folded, on
the front seat. Loosening his red tie, he then sprinted
through development backyards into the woods, to the
river. He moved along a high ridge till he could view the

dammed pool far below. The state troopers had arrived in record time.

The brown water bubbled as a diver finished his area search. A hand broke the surface and signaled toward the opposite bank.

State Police Marine Services Officers pushed a green polyethylene flat bottom boat into the river and rowed over to the diver. A rope was handed off and the diver submerged.

Paul became alert at this activity and needed to get closer. He crab walked slowly down the steep rocky embankment to get a better look at the scene below, keeping his silhouette minimal so he couldn't be seen and told to leave. He hoped his trousers wouldn't stain as he gradually crept down the almost vertical hill. The loose leaves were slippery and footing failed, flattening him on his back. Paul rapidly slid down and was unable to grasp anything as his fingers balled into fists. The right side of his head hit a large rock and his right leg folded. He didn't feel his femur protrude through his thigh as he crashed into a large basalt boulder. Paul became inert.

The marine officers looked up upon hearing the rustling of the leaves, but didn't see anything. Their focus returned to the water as the rope was tugged twice.

The boat returned to the bank, trailing the rope. Each volunteer grabbed a portion of the line and pulled. Whatever was at the end was slowly dragged through the mud. Part way out, the effort was halted. It was a rusty drive shaft from an old water turbine—nothing to do with the missing teenagers.

The divers finished the water search. The volunteers trampled along the bank and through the woods, without any more discoveries.

The work for the day ended. Davy admonished everyone not to discuss the day's events. All surged through the media waiting outside the gate. Davy announced a press conference at the Grand Cascades Lodge at five o'clock tomorrow night. Mayor Zicker, the police, Trooper Brown, and the corner would all be in attendance. Objections were loudly raised at the delay.

The reporters continued asking a silent Davy questions till he was in his car. He needed the time to organize and prepare what he could say based on the lack of evidence.

ೞೞೞ

In a small village, anything out of the ordinary became instantly noteworthy and a topic for endless discussion and gossip. Thanks to the current state of entertainment, murder and mayhem were common place and experienced every day and night through music, television, movies, and novels. Initial shock gave way to excitement over the media coverage the incidents were receiving. In town, everyone tried to be at the right place to be interviewed. Everyone had their own speculations. House parties were planned for these discussions. The absence of a few had brought many together. In the school corridors, the excited talk was all about the ongoing television coverage: what stations were represented, who saw on-air reporters, where they were, who was interviewed, and, only secondarily, the murder of Jud Robinson. The invincibility of the young shielded many from the possibility of personal danger. All were enjoying Hamburg's fifteen minutes of fame and wondering how they could cash in on it.

Ash nodded to Luna in English III, looking for some sign. Luna acknowledged him with a small smile. Ash's heart raced with this diminutive gesture.

Normally, this was one of Ash's favorite classes, especially now that they were discussing *The Weary Blues* by Langston Hughes. Blues poetry spoke to him of isolation, anguish, frustration, and the strong awareness of wanting to belong. However, his concentration wasn't in the lesson and its personal connections today. He needed to talk further with Luna.

Ash didn't want to lose any closeness he had tried to establish and was afraid his insistence on a meeting with Ephraim had done harm. After the period bell rang, he only had time to say "Hello" and "See you at lunch" as the students funneled through the door and raced to the next class. The rest of the morning classes droned on. Much of what each teacher espoused filled the room but did not evolve into any conscious thought.

After the last class before lunch, Ash found himself almost running to the cafeteria. He searched the large room—there she was, waiting for him at the same table. What sort of sign was this? *Was* this a sign?

At least she appeared to want to be with him, or perhaps she was just being polite and wanted to end their budding friendship personally. Ash quickly grabbed tomato soup and chilled fruit, raced to the table, and sat in front of Luna. "Hi, how are you?"

"Good."

"Everything going fine?"

"Yes. Do you know they have STEM league and academic team competition here?"

"No."

"I was wrong to think that there would be only yokels out here. I judge too quickly. And maybe you do too?"

"What do you mean?"

"This guy in the woods, what do you really know about him?"

"That he needs friends."

"That he needs friends or that you need friends?"

"What are you getting at?"

"I'm just saying that you shouldn't rush into things. You don't really know this person."

"I know how he feels."

"Again, how he feels or how you feel?"

"So you aren't going to meet him?"

"I didn't say that. I just need to know more. My mother was happy I found a friend so soon, but my father was closed lipped. Anything happen at the hospital?"

"Nothing, he just examined me. Does—does he think I'm a bully?"

"No, but maybe troubled."

"Did he say that?"

"No, I know how to read him."

"Well, I guess that's it then."

"There you go, jumping to conclusions again, Ash. I just need more information."

"About me?"

"Well, yes, and certainly about Ephron."

"His name is Ephraim. My given name is Korbin. I was born here and live here with my father and mother. I'm Goth because I like the mystique of the culture. I dress in black to align myself with a society I can identify with. I like horror literature. I am drawn to the occult and its religious imagery. I do not have any piercings or tattoos. You already knew most of this and now you know everything about me."

"I didn't mean for you to become upset."

"I'm not upset—I just thought you were a lot like me and would have a better understanding of me and especially how someone can really feel lonely."

"It's not you I'm really worried about. And I do know how it feels not to fit in—I've already told you that."

"But you haven't met Ephraim yet, and, after saying that, how could you judge people without any knowledge of them?"

"I'm not judging, just being cautious. By the way, what's his last name?"

"I don't know."

"So you don't know much about him and are going by assumptions based on a brief meeting."

"I don't really know you, but I can see you are a kind and decent person."

Ash moved a piece of pineapple around the paper pate with his plastic spoon. He had hoped so much to have another kindred soul, and now it seemed that he had alienated Luna with his insistence on meeting Ephraim.

"Have you called him?"

"Yes, two times, but he didn't answer."

"Leave a message?"

"He doesn't have voice recording on the phone."

"Wow, he is out of touch."

"Yes, and lonely. I didn't see a television or even a radio when I was there—doesn't mean he doesn't have one though, but I doubt it."

Luna scribbled in her ranch dressing with a carrot. "I—I don't even know if my father would allow me to go on a 'hike' with you."

"But I bet your mother would."

"I don't know. They both are upset over the murder. Dad doesn't talk much about his work, but this time he said the boy's face was completely missing. Now he's worried for my safety till this thing is resolved."

"Jud was an idiot and a bully! No one is sorry he's dead, believe me."

"Don't say that. I thought you valued all life."

Ash looked down, ashamed for his outburst and lack of faith. "I do, I do and you're right."

"You have to understand this is all very creepy to me. I'm new here. This is a lot to have happen in my first few days of being here."

"I do understand and, again, I'm sorry. I didn't mean to take life lightly and I know how hard it is for you."

Luna reached out and laid her hand over his. "Ash, I really do think you mean well and, and I'm really happy that I met you."

"Yeah, well, it's okay. You don't have to meet him."

Luna looked directly into Ash's eyes and saw something that called out to her. Perhaps it was her reflection, perhaps a trapped soul—it was something she couldn't ignore. "Clearly, this means so much to you, and you are so sure that this Ephraim is harmless that maybe we can work something out."

Ash couldn't stop his smile from growing. He placed his other hand on Luna's. "Thank you, thank you. I knew you are truly a kind soul."

Luna slowly slipped her hand from between his and rose. "Why don't you call me and we can discuss this more?"

Ash stood. "Sure, sure. That'll be great."

In that moment, life became good.

☙❧☙

Bad news greeted Jay the next morning. The desk of-ficer called out as soon as the sergeant entered the station.

"Sarg, Sarg! June Armstead called early this morning reporting her husband missing."

"What?"

"Paul Armstead didn't come home last night and he wasn't at work yesterday."

"Shit!"

"Think this is tied to his daughter's disappearance?"

"Crap! I don't know." Jay shook his head. Every-thing was rapidly falling apart. "Even if it's not, it comes at a bad time. Shit!"

"Mrs. Armstead was really upset."

"Yeah, I'll bet. She home?"

"She had me call her neighbor, but then the neighbor called and told me her condition was near a breakdown so I notified Emergency and they picked her up. She's at St. Clair's."

"Okay. Call Hines in here. We have some canvas work to do."

Jay was waiting for Hines in the parking lot stomp-ing his feet to keep warm as he re-read his notes from the interview.

Hines came to a stop beside Jay and opened the patrol car passenger door. "Jesus, were does this end, Sarg?"

"Not at a good place, Ned."

"Well, where do we start?"

"I saw him yesterday morning at the crime scene. He wanted to get to the search area. Davy sent him away. So we'll start there and trace his route to work."

"Which is where?"

"He works as an executive advisor for 3County Financial Security, a registered investment firm on Route 23. Keep your eyes out for a late model white Toyota 4Runner."

The drive produced nothing unusual, no sign of the car, and no pertinent data at 3County.

"Ned, let's stop by the hospital and see how Mrs. Armstead is doing."

Doctor Brenson was on call. He met the men in the emergency room and escorted them to his office.

"How is June Armstead doing, Doc?"

"She's sedated at the moment."

"When do you think we can question her?"

"Not today, perhaps tomorrow."

"Any news about the Robinson kid?"

"He did die of blunt force trauma. Estimated time of death, sometime last night. No signs of defense so either he knew the assailant and didn't expect an attack, or he was completely surprised."

"'Knew the assailant, huh?'"

"Or was surprised."

"Could a woman have the strength to demolish his face?"

"I couldn't speculate on that, Sergeant. However, rage and adrenalin can augment strength, so it is possible a female could inflict that much damage."

"Okay. Thanks, Doc. We'll be here tomorrow."

On the way out to the patrol car, the officers were approached by a reporter with a barrage of questions, hoping one would produce information. "Any news on the murder? Why are you here? Has there been another discovery? What did the autopsy reveal?"

"We can't answer any question in this continuing investigation. Thank you."

The reporter was left at the hospital entrance, still holding his microphone out, still hoping for answers.

"Do you think the girl did this, Sarg, and then ran away?" Hines asked.

"That would be too easy an explanation, Corporal, and it doesn't solve the other missing teenagers."

"Yeah, but what if she did and met up with her father. That would explain his disappearance as well. Maybe he's protecting her."

"I don't think it's that neat, and Paul Armstead would have communicated with his wife."

"Well, where do we go now?"

"Head toward Bluffs Court. We'll search around there."

A couple of houses from Paul's residence, they stopped to investigate a white Toyota parked along the road. The doors were locked. A jacket and tie were carefully folded on the front seat.

Hines called the license in. The car belonged to Paul Armstead.

"Let's try his house, maybe he's home now."

Hines followed the sergeant as they walked to the house.

No one answered the front door.

"Go around the back, Corporal, and take a look."

Hines returned shortly. "Nothing amiss. No sign of entry or anything suspicious."

Jay stepped out on the lawn and surveyed the area.

"He can't be far." Turning around, he stopped north and stared at the wood's edge. "That's the ridge over the Wallkill, near the mill."

"Yeah," Hines replied.

"Let's have a look."

The two covered the distance in a short period of time. Hines stepped into the leading edge of the tree line and almost slipped down as the field abruptly ended.

"Wow, that quite a steep incline!"

Below was the river and farther up the river was the damn.

"That's where we found the car and body, isn't it?"

"Yeah, Corporal, let's walk the edge. Be careful."

They paused directly above the pool.

"Look at that," Jay indicated some disturbance in the leaves and shrubs between two large oak trees.

"Could be an animal trail." Hines bent down to inspect it, not really knowing what he was looking for.

"See anything below, Corporal?"

Hines leaned forward and almost lost his balance. Jay quickly grabbed his holster belt and pulled him back.

"It's too dangerous from here, Corporal, and this area was searched before we discovered the car. Let's go back. I'll get Harper to tow the car back to the station and have someone assigned to canvas the neighborhood just in case someone saw something."

CHAPTER 13

Still clothed, Ephraim awoke with a purpose and rushed to the basement. He retrieved the two buckets of skins and carried them to a spigot outside. He emptied the liquid and rinsed the skins till all the mixture was removed. Inside the barn, he searched the left wall for the drying studs. He squeezed out the excess water and, for now, hung the body and head pieces to drip dry.

Back in the basement, Ephraim rolled the carcass off the table onto a blue canvas. The dead meat made a thick beefy sound as it hit the floor. Bundling it up, he slung it over his shoulder and struggled up the steps as it dragged behind him. There wasn't time to bury it now so he deposited the load inside the iron fence surrounding the family cemetery, reassured that it was in a secured place. He came back with the hands and feet and slid the bucket under the tarp then shut the gate, not thinking to latch it.

Breathing heavily, he waddled to the kitchen for the brain slurry and towels. Back in the barn, he placed the human hides between two towels and squeezed, repeating the process with new dry cloths till the moisture was removed. He carefully patted Angelina's long light hair then smeared the brain mixture on the inside of the skins, making sure every area was covered while removing any fat or muscle tissue left. After a thorough gentle rubbing to force the solution into the tissues, Ephraim rolled up each piece and returned to the kitchen to store the two damp piles in the refrigerator to let the brain solution truly soak in.

He sat in the chair facing the window to catch his breath and plan the next process. He needed a frame for the body. Brew always helped his thinking so Ephraim put some Typhoo Tea on to steep. Where could he obtain a human form to mount Angelina's skin? The smell of tea brought memories. He slid off the chair and headed to the father's den. Ephraim turned the swirl brass knob and pushed the double doors open. The air inside had no smell, no substance, just stagnant age. The silence of the room was entrapped by absence of life. The interior seemed melancholy: gray distempered walls; a baroque desk, covered with meaningless objects; dusty Mahoney shelves, supporting outdated medical books; three faded yellow cushions on wicker chairs; aged dark green velvet drapes, covering three windows; black double metal sconces with candelabra bulbs; and a six-light chandelier, hanging in the room's middle. A large brick fireplace with an outsized dark granite mantel remained unused. Black and white photos of fox hunting and long-dead fierce-looking men adorned the walls. Above the desk in an ornate golden frame was a large copy of George Jennison's portrait of a vacant-looking balding man with a brown drooping mustache and gray beard in a be-medaled red uniform with ermine cape: King Edward VII, eldest son of Queen Victoria. And in the far corner was what Ephraim had braved entrance into the father's place for: a life-sized male anatomy model. The exposed numbered organs were the only colorful thing in the den. It would be the perfect form for Angelina. All he had to do was cut out the genitals. The existing hands and feet of the figure would make up for what had been sacrificed. The father had finally helped him!

Ephraim hugged the model, careful not to let the internal parts fall out and wrestled it out of the den to the cellar.

It was now early afternoon. He returned to the kitchen, the one room where he spent most of his time. He realized how hungry he was. In the cupboard, Ephraim found the jars of Marmite. After toasting pieces of rye bread, he spread a thin layer of the brown yeast extract on each then added slices of cheddar cheese. The mouth-burning effect brought warm recollections. Uncle had always added a teaspoon of it to soups, stews, and casseroles. Since it wasn't readily available in the grocery store, Uncle had it delivered from the Healthy Place food store in large quantities. It was one of the few good memories Ephraim retained.

He rubbed his palms, not only in anticipation of the work that was ahead, but because of the chill in the air. He made a hot drink from Cadbury's cocoa powder and made a mental note to check the furnace.

Angelina's covering wouldn't be ready till tomorrow. Ephraim used the down time to clean up and get ready for Angelina's rebirth. He repositioned the Persian carpet, hosed down the steel table, emptied the bucket in the sink, and rinsed his knives. After rolling the anatomy model onto the table, he removed the stand and then cut out the genital representation leaving a moderate opening. He threw the stand into the furnace with several shovels of coal, then, using fine sandpaper smoothed the edges of the hole. Satisfied everything was done that could be done for now, Ephraim only had to check on the refrigerator contents. The gel had set and the prepared bundles were intact.

It had been a busy day so far. The sun had started its farewell. Tonight, Ephraim would have an onion and mayonnaise sandwich, his favorite, and a tall glass of chilled ginger beer for dinner. Now, he would relax and settle in the parlor to read Mary Shelly's *Frankenstein*.

exex

Bill Corning had strategically placed reader boards providing navigation to the Silver Spring Conference Room 1 at hall intersections of the Grand Cascades Lodge. The turnout of reporters, cameras, and concerned citizens was too large for the room—the meeting had to be moved to the bigger Conference Room 2.

Special Agent Davy, Lieutenant Soldering, and Sergeant Hurray sat behind a podium on the audience's right, Mayor Zicker, Doctor Brenson, Trooper Brown, and Superintendent Bronner sat on the left. Davy, Soldering, and Hurray whispered together. The mayor smoothed his hair, though he knew every brown strand was in place. He didn't cross his legs or fidget. Arthur Zicker belonged in front of people. Brenson seemed concerned. He was always uneasy when bad news was to be delivered. Trooper Brown sat stoic. The superintendent reviewed the talking points for his part.

All stared straight ahead as reporters claimed first-row chairs, camera equipment was set up, the back rows occupied, and standing room filled.

Davy stood after everyone calmed down and attention was focused forward. He started with a traditional, but inappropriate introduction, "Welcome and thank for your concern in this matter." He shifted his feet and glanced at his notes, now aware of this lame statement. He wasn't projecting authority and moved on to recover.

"I'm FBI Special Agent James Davy—to my left is Lieutenant Mark Soldering and Sergeant Jay Hurray, first investigator. On my right are Mayor Arthur Zicker, Coroner Clark Brenson, State Trooper David Brown, and Superintendent Don Bronner. In conjunction with local and state officials, the FBI is aiding in the investigation of the disappearance of four young Hamburg people, all within a short period of time. This meeting is to inform you of our progress so far. I want to assure you that we are not holding back on any relevant information that the public needs to know."

Before he could continue, a loud voice from the front row shouted, "What do you mean by 'relevant'? Are you holding back *some* facts?"

"As you should know, since this is an ongoing investigation, I can not reveal any information that may, in some way, jeopardize the outcome of the investigation. This is standard practice and does not mean we are hiding any facts that need to be known."

Another front-row voice followed, "Is it true that an adult is now missing too?"

"You will be told everything if you allow us to continue."

No further questions were issued.

Davy continued, "Let me recap what has happened and where we are. Two former Wallkill High School students, Vincent Marconi and Dawn Portny were reported missing during the last week of October. Shortly after, two current students, Jud Robinson and Brenda Arm-stead, were also reported missing. Sergeant Hurray confirmed that these persons were indeed missing and their whereabouts unknown. We have since found one of the four, Jud Robinson. He apparently died from a severe beating to his face and, while in his car, was pushed into the Wallkill River."

"Do we have a serial killer?"

"Please, please, let us finish and, if you still have questions, we will answer them. Doctor Brenson, will you please provide more information about Jud Robinson's injuries?"

"Certainly." Brenson approached the podium and placed his notes on the angled platform. "Jud Robinson died from blunt force trauma, not from suffocation. He was deceased before the car entered the river pool. Deaths resulting from blunt force, which is an impact with a dull, hard surface or object, are the most common cause of trauma deaths. In this case, this cutaneous blunt force injury can be typed as avulsion. This is a severe form of laceration, in which skin, muscles, and bone are ripped away from normal areas of connections. In simple terms, his face was pulverized by an unknown heavy object. This was a homicide."

A ripple of noise spread throughout the audience at the word "homicide."

Davy rose. "Thank you Doctor Brenson. Next is Lieutenant Soldering."

"In answer to your previous question, as of this time, we are not labeling this as a serial killing. Until we know the outcome of our investigation into the other three involved, we are treating this is a single murder episode. We cannot ascertain any common motive or relationship. There is no reason to rush into a headline-grabbing scenario. Sergeant Hurray will fill you in further."

Jay stood and read from a prepared document. "After notification of possible missing persons, we performed on-site inquiries and obtained contact information of friends and acquaintances who might know possible locations for these individuals. After this part of the inquiry, we determined that the involved were indeed missing. We attained warrants for cell phone data, personal effects, and living areas. These produced no useful information. We are in the process of executing a detailed and thorough investigation that will resolve this situation and not cause prejudice of problems for prosecution.

"To date, we have recovered Jud Robinson. A scarf was discovered near the murder scene at the old mill and identified as belonging to Brenda Armstead. Her father, Paul, is now also missing. His jacket and tie were found in his car near his house. The car has been retrieved for forensics. So the answer to your question is 'Yes' there is a missing adult. As of this moment, we don't how, or if, these incidences are connected. Thank you." The sergeant sat down.

The audience produced another buzz of noise.

Trooper Brown approached the microphone. "The recovered 1965 Ford Galaxie will be taken to the Sussex Barracks and minutely searched for trace fibers, hair, and impressions. Any materials found or photographed will be sent to the Office of Forensic Sciences for analysis in Little Falls, New Jersey. The Special Investigations Section, especially the Violent Criminal Apprehension Program, will cooperate with and coordinate, if necessary, between law enforcement agencies during this period." The trooper went back to his seat.

Mayor Zicker unconsciously patted the graying hair on the sides of his head as he stepped up to the podium. He appraised the audience then gave them his best political smile. He slowly surveyed the room, more to show his profile to everyone than view the seated. The mayor was in his element. With arms lifted high, Zicker boomed, "Ladies and gentlemen, I assure you that everything is under control.

"We have the finest FBI agents and our own superb police department on these incidents. It is only a matter of time before all is sorted out. One tragedy doesn't produce a crisis. We don't know what the situation is with the others. For now, let's keep Jud Robinson in our prayers and keep good thoughts for the others. We must not let this become worse by speculation and rumor. Normalcy is the key to enduring these misfortunes. Together, as a united community—" At this point, the mayor clasped his hands in a ball and shook them for effect. "—we can get through this. My office door is always open to my constituents. As Winston Churchill aptly said, 'we have nothing to fear, but fear itself.'" For good measure, Arthur finished with, "We will overcome!"

Satisfied with his short, poignant speech, the mayor turned to Superintendent Bronner, who took this as a cue to address the group. He stood behind the podium and positioned the microphone—so reminiscent of countless assemblies—cleared his throat, and waited for a plausible silence. "Student and staff safety has always been a vital topic in our district. The well being of our students is foremost in procedures and daily activities. To this, we patrol the hallways hourly and ensure all outside entries are secure. We have added extra crossing guards and solicited volunteers to oversee bus stops. We have brought in psychologists for the elementary, middle, and high schools to deal with any questions or concerns our students may have.

"We are inviting The State Department of Education, Advocates for Children of New Jersey, Safe Kids New Jersey, and other organizations in to give safety and instructional presentations for all our students. More importantly, we will continue to provide a normal atmosphere within our school district. I assure you that coming, being in school, and returning home will be a safe experience." Bronner returned to his seat.

Special Agent Davy asked the question he didn't want to ask, "Any questions?"

Immediately, the room erupted with shouts and flaying arms to gain attention.

"Do you believe Brenda Armstead is dead?"

"Are Vincent Marconi and Dawn Portny considered adults?"

"Do you think Paul Armstead had anything to do with this?"

"Do you have any suspects?"

"How did the parents react?"

"Where do you go from here?"

"If this is not a serial killing, how do you explain so many disappearances in such a short time?"

"What exactly could cause the massive damage to Jud's face?"

Davy answered each question the best he could, referring to others when needed. After a decent length of time, he ended the conference. "Thank you. We will be touch when we have more to offer." Then he herded the group through a back door.

TV reporters claimed spots in the room and began reporting. Townspeople grouped in the hall and outside the building, analyzing everything said.

At the mayor's office, the group discussed the conference. Zicker went straight to the core. "So we have one dead and no clues or suspects, unless you want to throw in Armstead."

"So far, Mayor, yes," Davy answered.

"Well, what will we have for the next press conference?"

"Nothing's been scheduled."

"Not yet, but there will be demands. This doesn't look good for the town, gentlemen, not at all."

Soldering and Jay understood that that "town" meant the mayor.

"Look more into Armstead. Find his history, dig for anything that might point to sadistic behavior. We can't let this slide. Action is paramount. Interview acquaintances and friends of the missing. Put everyone on the force on this and call in more troopers if necessary. We need to find something, fast."

Davy didn't like this shift of control. "I assure you that we are covering all aspects of this, Mayor."

"Okay, I'll not keep you from further work." Mayor Zicker dismissed everyone.

In the hall, Davy commented, "This may be a case where we rely on a mistake the killer makes."

"You mean, we'll have to wait till someone gets killed again?"

"Could be. For now, let's concentrate on finding Armstead."

The group marched out in uncertainty.

ᗑᗑᗑ

Ephraim awoke to a feeling of a long gone Christmas morning. Quickly dressing, he rushed to the kitchen, gathered the gelatin molds and skins, and hurried to the cellar as fast as his burdens and short legs allowed.

Placing his refrigerated cache on the table next to the plastic model, he turned on the light, for better vision in the close work to come, and rewound the Victrola, replacing the "Pachelbel Cannon" with "Suite for Solo Cello No. 1 in G Major" by Johann Bach. The symmetrical cycle of low soothing sounds filled the basement and his entire being with mournful yet hopeful music. It was a wonderful morning.

Ephraim carefully spread out the body skin and head cap and lightly towel dried what remained of the subcutaneous layers. They required some moisture, though, to be pliable and then, as they dried, the skin would tighten around the anatomy model.

He nestled a soup bowl gel into each breast pocket, needing only to shave a little off the right mold. They both looked good and felt better. He stuffed the storage container gel mold into the hole he had made in the model and cored out a shaft. He would rework it as necessary, depending on the fit later.

Gently picking up the body skin, Ephraim layered it over the front of the model. He smoothed out wrinkles and unnatural looking lumps and folds on the body, arms, and legs. It was as easy as dressing a doll.

He carefully rolled the model over and, ever so tenderly, began to push the edges of the torso skin together with the palms of his hands. The male model was larger than Angelina, but through persistence, Ephraim managed to stretch the hide and meet the edges.

He retrieved cat gut and a curved needle from the cabinet then slowly, starting at the neck, sewed together the body seam with a tight overcast stitch till he reached the buttocks. He stuffed a small amount of excelsior into each cheek cavity and ended above the anus tying the line off with a tailor's knot. Ephraim repeated the procedure with each arm and leg.

Next, he fitted the face and hair on the model and stitched the back seem. The bottom didn't quite reach to the body skin, but jewelry or a scarf would cover that.

Ephraim stepped back preparing himself for the reveal, for the rebirth. Uncle would have done a better job, but this surely would do.

He turned Angelina back on her back.

Ephraim remained motionless at what he saw. A scarecrow face grinned at him. Damp lengths of hair spiked from the head. The flat painted eyes were almost hidden by sagging lids. Her compressed nose was crooked and her lips distended and irregular. Stretch marks lined the body. Despite his best efforts, plastic organs budged against the tight wrapping, and pink plastic hands and feet protruded from graying skin.

This was not Angelina! After all his work and hopes, he had created a lifeless Frankenstein!

Ephraim backed up, away from his creation in despair, away from failure. No, no this couldn't be. He looked around the basement for help, for a sign of what to do, for Uncle. Ephraim turned away from what lay on the table. The music was not soothing anymore. It now scolded him in repetitive low reprimands for trying to be someone he could not be. He abruptly brushed aside the tonearm of the Victrola causing the soundbox to emit a loud irritating scratch. He needed silence to consider what to do next. Ephraim slapped the sides of his head.

"Think, think!"

His eyes rested on the beech cabinet, on the top left drawer. He opened it. Next to the tray of glass eyes were paint and makeup. "Yes, yes!"

He removed the contents. He had witness Uncle make his mounts come alive though applying these materials. He used red for the lips, talcum powder on the face, and rouge for the cheeks then combed her hair.

When he finished, the result was passable. After lunch, he would try to remove the painted eyes and implant glass ones somehow. He breathed a sigh of relief.

Darkness met him in the hallway. The day had slipped past, and it was evening now, but the gloom of November didn't affect Ephraim's mood. Happiness revisited him as he now prepared for a late supper of vegetable soup and buttered bread.

When Ephraim returned, Angelina's skin had darkened and stiffened. She did not look well, but perhaps she was suitable. He climbed on top of the table and over her. Her breasts were supple enough to give him an erection.

Ephraim took off his pants and tried to position himself. The plastic legs were immovable—he wasn't able to reach the gelatin mold.

Depression flooded his being. Failure wouldn't go away.

"All for naught. I have lost! I have lost again!"

He rolled off the table onto the floor, sat in misery, and started to cry. He couldn't remember the last time he cried, and this thought brought more sorrow. He cried for his mother, for Angelina, for his Uncle, and finally for himself. After a while, Ephraim stood and pulled his trousers on. Angelina would have to leave again. He opened the furnace and shoveled coal. Leaving the gate open, he maneuvered Angelina off the table and dragged her to the opening. Lifting her head on the gate, he moved the feet, lifted, and pushed the form diagonally through the opening into the fire. Burnt hair, melting plastic, and crisp skin odors leaked from the furnace and filled the entire house. Ephraim was too despondent to notice. It took a long while to dispose of his failure. He had to bank the coal several times, as the embers were covered in layers of bubbling plastic.

He turned off the lights and went upstairs. He wasn't Uncle. He didn't have Uncle's skills—he didn't have skills at all and, now, he didn't have Angelina. The silence, the empty house were tangible signs of his loneliness.

In the kitchen, he looked out the window toward the

swamp. It was too dark to see where the red had been and if it was back, but perhaps Angelina was back near that building. Yes, perhaps she was! Hope made despair weak and optimism visited once again. Ephraim put on a navy wool pea coat and hurried to the barn where he found a three-pound double-faced sledge hammer and placed it on the passenger seat of the car. He had Ash's directions in the glove box then headed out along the driveway.

The gate was open. He had forgotten to close it, but that didn't matter now. He was journeying out to find his true love and this made him somebody—he was Don Quixote in search of Dulcinea.

The sleek, elongated Buick eased through the night in a sleepy Hamburg. All had retired, safe inside from the evil that was loose outside. No one in town saw the char-coal car with tinted windows as it silently moved through their lives.

The Hamburg Police had five square miles to patrol with only two vehicles. The little luck Ephraim had was with him that night for a while.

He had little trouble arriving at Gingerbread Castle Road. The road was deserted—all the reporters were now at the Grand Cascades Lodge waiting. Ephraim slowed, concentrating on finding the mill access road. He noticed a light gray Honda Pilot parked in the back of the aban-doned lot across from the Ginger Bread Castle entrance. On his left was the access road, but yellow tape had been strung across the entrance preventing entry for him to

Angelina. Disappointed, he rode past and turned around on Bluffs Court.

Hope again shut out the gloom of depression as he neared the parking lot. Perhaps Angelina had moved to a new location. She never seemed to be in the same place twice. He slowed, shut off his lights, and turned into the nearest part of the lot.

Getting out, he observed the car: foggy windows, rocking, and, as he approached, muffled noises. These were the signs! This was the pattern! Angelina had left but had returned once again. Grabbing the hammer, he silently moved closer.

Angelina should be on the right side so he needed to eliminate the aggressor on the left. Ephraim opened the driver's door, his hammer raised, and then froze. A man and a boy, both naked, were sweating and hugging each other. Their faces were a mixture of horror and embarrassment as they stared at him.

Ephraim slammed the door shut and quickly hobbled back to his car. He pulled out of the lot and sped home, through the open gate, into the barn. In his bedroom, he hid under the covers and tried to comprehend what he had witnessed. What were they doing? They saw him! Where was Angelina? All the markers were there. He didn't understand and was frightened. Maybe morning would bring clarity. For now, he didn't feel safe. The world outside the manor was now more confusing and frightening. Ephraim longed for the solitude of the old days.

ɷɷ

Hines had asked the grangers for help in searching the neighbor, while he would visit nearby houses to question the occupants.

He gathered them at Bluffs Court.

"Okay, gentlemen and ladies, we are now looking for a middle aged man who may have been or is still in this vicinity. As before, shout out if you come across anything suspicious, whatever that may be. We'll search the neighborhood first. Do not enter any house, garage, or outbuildings. If you suspect anything, I will ask for the owner's permission. We will start at the west end and work toward the River."

As the group neared the location of the white car, Hines gathered everyone. "We determined that this was the last known spot where Mr. Armstead was. His white Toyota was found here, locked with his jacket and tie inside. Again, please be respectful of property, but be thorough in this area."

The group swarmed through the remaining yards, over fences, and through hedge rows. Hines knocked on doors nearby and those that opened provided no information. He calmed people who came out to complaint about the intrusion. It was near dusk when the grangers marched across the field to the woods.

At the edge of the trees lining the steep river bank, Hines again addressed the searchers. "I almost fell on the leafy slope, so be very careful and remain within arm's length of each other. We will proceed down and then move north along the river and up the hill and continue like this till we are a half mile upstream."

Not more than ten feet down, a shout went out. A granger pointed to a boulder twenty more feet down. A body was crumpled against a boulder.

"Okay. Everyone, halt."

Hines gingerly slide down, holding to branches and small trees. The corporal recognized Armstead and death.

"Everyone, back up. We're finished."

Hines dismissed the group and called EMS, Davey, Jay, and Soldering.

CHAPTER 14

Ash and Luna agreed to tell their parents they were going to the mall in Wantage with some friends. The Brensons hesitated at first, but since Luna was traveling with company and away from Hamburg, they relented. Ash's mother was happy he had a group of friends. She talked with Henry and both agreed to let him drive her maroon Honda CRV that morning.

"Did you call your friend?" Luna asked.

"Yes, but he didn't answer."

"Maybe he's not home."

Ash shrugged. "He doesn't have anywhere to go. He'll be there."

Ash felt in fine spirits as he drove Route 23 with Luna beside him. Secretly, he thought of this as a date. There wasn't much to see on the short trip. Autumn had stripped trees clean and spread colors of tan and brown throughout the countryside. For a mid-November day, the temperature was mild.

Both had removed their jackets. Ash advised on dressing less gothic so Ephraim wouldn't be confused. Both had toned down on their facial makeup. Luna wore a black short shirt and a vintage gray blouse, unaware of what lay ahead. They rolled the windows down a bit to enjoy the unseasonably warm breeze on their way to this adventure.

"We have to go through Sussex. It's smaller than Hamburg, but I hear they are getting a Taco Bell."

Luna looked out the window at nothing in particular, enjoying the freedom of the ride.

Damn! Ash realized that, once again, he was making an ass of himself. Why did he do this every time he was with Luna?

"I've brought my Wiccan altar set. I thought we could form the coven today."

Lana appeared not to have listened.

"Ah, here we are." Ash was finally glad to turn onto Hankins Road. "It's just down here a bit. There!" He pointed to the iron-gated driveway ahead set into the wood edge. "And it's open."

"Are you really sure of this, Ash?"

"Yes. More than ever. Wicca asks us to respect all

life-affirming events. This is one and don't you see the pattern in this? I was lonely and I found you. Ephraim was apart from life and found me and now he will find you too. Just don't act afraid when you see Ephraim. He's very sensitive about his looks." Ash came to a stop in front of the barn. "All right. I think he's usually in the kitchen. I'll knock on the door."

Luna followed behind.

"Ephraim, Ephraim, it's Ash. I told you I'd come back and I've brought a friend."

They waited for a response.

"Maybe try the front door, Ash."

As both turned, the kitchen door opened a crack.

"Ash?" Ephraim called.

"Yes, do you remember me?"

"Certainly. You—you brought another?"

"Yes, my friend Luna. She wants to meet you."

The door opened wider. Luna could see a large eye peering out.

"A female?"

"Yes."

"Is she your pusher?"

"Pusher?" Aside to Luna, Ash whispered, "See I told you he speaks strange."

"Ah, does she belong to you, Ash?"

"No, we are just good friends."

His eye looked over Luna and brightened when he saw the red car behind her. Last night and his longing for solitude was quickly forgotten. Angelina had returned and so quickly! The door opened wider.

"Ash, it is good to see you again."

"Can we come in, Ephraim?"

"Oh, yes. I apologize for my poor manners. Please enter."

Luna frowned as an acrid smell met them when they entered the kitchen. Ephraim was standing by a window with his back to the door.

"Ephraim, it's all right. Luna won't be frightened, will you, Luna?"

"No, no."

Ephraim slowly turned around, looking at the floor.

Ash was startled again at his features. Luna involuntarily brought her hand to her mouth. A cry died in her throat.

Silence seemed to last longer than its time. Ephraim finally looked up, at Luna. "You don't find me horrible?"

Luna tried to hide her initial shock. "No, no. Not at all."

Ephraim became emboldened. "She is beautiful, Ash. Dark, not like Angelina, but beautiful."

Luna felt his eyes as they surveyed her and wondered who Angelina was.

"Is the red automobile yours?"

"Yes, we drove out," Ash answered.

Ephraim again studied Luna—dark clothed, long green streaked black hair, pretty, small breasts—so different from his Angelinas, but this one was here of her own free will, and there was the red car, but in daylight. And Ash—Ephraim didn't know the other males. He worked through his confusion and reasoned his way out. The pattern was a variation, but only slightly. Then again, each time Angelina had come to him was different. Perhaps if this one could be kept alive, his problems would be solved.

"How have you been, Ephraim?"

Ash's question broke into Ephraim's thoughts. He reluctantly turned to Ash.

"I have managed, Ash. Thank you for your inquiry. Again, you must excuse my manners. Would you like some brew?"

Ash whispered to Luna, "Tea."

Luna had regained her composure and was adjusting to the situation to the point of feeling empathy with Ephraim. "Yes. Thank you. That would be nice."

He seemed so polite.

"Please, please have seat." Ephraim pulled chairs from the porcelain table and bustled around the kitchen. "Please, please have seat."

"So what have you been doing lately?" Ash inquired.

The question caused Ephraim to drop a cup. It fragmented on the red and white checked linoleum floor.

"Blimey!"

"Let me help." Luna began to pick up the pieces. "Do you have dust pan and broom?"

"Yes, yes, I do." Ephraim rushed to the closet and re-trieved an oak dust pan and horse hair brush. "Will this be appropriate?"

"Yes." Luna reached for the offered items. Her hand touched Ephraim's.

Ephraim froze at the contact. He could smell flowers and sense the softness of her delicate skin. She was not afraid of him—she did not find him repulsive as the oth-ers had. This new transformation of Angelina could mean the end of the cycle of departures.

He stared at the petite figure before him.

"Ephraim, Ephraim, you all right?"

"Yes, Ash, I am." Ephraim turned his gaze to Ash and suddenly felt sorry for his only friend.

ᏭᎾᏭᎾ

The hastily called press conference drew the same large crowd of reporters and town people. Mayor Zicker, Agent Davy, Lieutenant Soldering, Sergeant Hurray, and Doctor Brenson sat behind the podium.

The mayor stood and assumed his best political pos-ture. "As I assured you a short time ago, I would inform you of events as they happened. Our police department has been very diligent and methodical throughout this entire investigation and it has begun to pay off. Today Mr. Paul Armstead's body was discovered on a ridge above Wallkill River."

Questions erupted from the audience and merged into an excited rumble of noise and activity as hand-held cameras moved into positions. Yelling reporters stood or held up arms and pointed pens, as if these gestures would single them out for acknowledgement.

"Again, questions will be answered later. Please be calm while we continue."

Zicker turned and nodded to Davy.

Special Agent Davy moved to the microphone. "After a canvas and search of the neighborhood where Mr. Armstead's car was discovered, his body was found lying against a large boulder, apparently the result of a fall. Early forensics of his car did not reveal any signs of forced entry. Mr. Armstead apparently placed his jacket and tie in the car before locking it. Keys were found on his person. Based on his earlier actions, we think Armstead was trying to view the activities in the area below where the scarf of his daughter, Brenda, was found. This is a tragic accident and that is all it is. The cause of death is not related to the Robinson murder. Dr. Brenson will address this."

Dr. Brenson stood. "Paul Armstead suffered from exposure and a broken femur that pierced his right buttock, which subsequently caused chronic venous insufficiency. Blood pooled in his leg veins resulting in a condition called stasis. This lack of blood movement led to a swollen right leg. Livor mortis and rigor mortis place the time of death near the time Mr. Armstead was reported missing. There were no signs or indication of a struggle or fight."

Davey then fielded questions till they became repetitive.

"Keep up the work. We need this to conclude soon," Mayor Zicker whispered to the group as they left the room. "If nothing else, come up with a reasonable excuse for the disappearance of the first two, and a probable scenario for Brenda Armstead's absence, since we only have a hysterical woman to deal with now."

Special Agent Davy stopped and watched the back of the retreating mayor, not wanting to process what he had heard.

Jay grabbed Davy's upper right arm, "Ignore him, James. His mouth sometimes is faster than his brain. We'll get to the end of this the correct way."

෧෨෧

Ephraim poured water into the kettle. The embers in the stove were cooling. "Oh dear, I am afraid I am out of fuel and I have been remiss in banking the fire."

"Want me to help?" Ash asked.

"There are cords of fuel near the barn."

"I'll get some." Ash had left before Luna could protest.

Ephraim was happy to be alone with Luna, but he didn't know what to do, how to be social. He poked in the stove to provide air to what remained of the fire and addressed Luna without facing her. "Do you read?"

"Yes."

"What do you read?"

Luna listed novel titles and then commented about the beauty of the woods and about the goodness of life, unconsciously using words as a barrier between them.

Ephraim felt at ease with her, misreading her friendliness. He moved toward her—each step sending a pleasant tremor throughout his body as he neared.

Ash came back too soon with an armload of split wood. "Been busy outside?"

"Pardon?"

"I noticed some digging near the fenced-in area and a blue tarp on the ground inside. Is it a cemetery?"

Ephraim again froze—the hole containing his first love—the canvas covering his failure. Did these reveal anything to Ash? It seemed Ash hadn't disturbed them, yet, but did Ash see something he would remember later? Why did he let Ash into his world? Uncle had been correct about outsiders, but, through Ash, Angelina had come back and then now she had found him once again through Ash. And this time she was alive and inviting. He felt grateful to Ash and sorry for what must come. It was so difficult dealing with the outside.

For now he had to think, think. Ephraim wanted to pound the side of his head, but quickly thought better of it. He must not show concern. Ash could not suspect anything at this moment. Later, it would not matter.

"Oh, it is…I have been…putting in a garden. I was planting flowers to honor my Uncle who is interred within the fence boundaries."

"Planting a garden in November?"

Ephraim felt panic and sat uneasily, trying not to rock back and forth. "I—I needed to soften the ground for spring planting. The canvas covers compost material."

"Oh, okay. Are you all right, Ephraim? You look disturbed."

"I am well, but I think I need more fuel for the stove. I will retrieve it."

"I'll get more, no problem."

"No, no. You are a guest." Ephraim hurried out the door. He shambled out toward the fence.

Ash watched him scramble across the overgrown lawn then turned. "So what do you think about Ephraim, Luna?"

"I don't know. He is unusual and deformed. I don't like the way he looks at me. This place has a queer smell about it. There's something unsettling here. I don't know. I think I'd like to leave soon. You know, no one knows where we are!"

"Yes, yes. But do you see how he needs friends? He's all alone out here. I smell something too, but it's an old house near a swamp. He's probably never seen or talked to a girl before, especially a pretty one like you." Ash hoped the compliment added to his argument.

"Please, let's stay just a little longer. I want to explain Wicca to him and to you and get to know him better."

"You already have explained Wicca to me. We could save Wicca for another time, don't you think?"

"It won't take long, trust me, and I want to show you both some rituals. You'll feel good after the ceremony and good about making friends with Ephraim later. After all, you are a good person."

Luna took in the compliment and agreed to remain for just a while longer.

While Ash and Luna talked, Ephraim reached the family cemetery. The gate was open and the tarp had apparently been blown into a corner exposing bare ground. He gripped the fence to keep from falling down. Angelina's old body was gone! He franticly looked around. Nothing was in sight. Where did it go? It—it could not have walked on its own. Who took it? His safe surroundings had again been violated. Things were getting worse. The bucket remained unseen under part of the canvas—hands and feet still in it. Ephraim emptied the contents into the swamp. The feet plunged straight into the dark water—the hands glided down, crab-like. He threw the bucket into the barn. He returned to the kitchen, confused, and now uncertain.

"Where's the wood?"

"What?"

"You went out for more wood."

"Yes, yes, how silly of me. I forgot my mission

completely. I—I was checking the compost hole to ascertain if any animals had been grubbing around."

"I put some wood in fire box. I think the water is boiling now."

"Yes, yes. Thank you. Let us enjoy some char. Please sit down. Luna, may I call you Luna for now?"

"Certainly, Ephraim." Something sounded wrong with the request, but the thought quickly dispersed.

"Excellent. Thank you." Ephraim poured tea. "Do you prefer sugar or milk or perhaps both?"

"A spoonful of sugar would be great."

Ephraim produced a crock with brown sugar and offered it to Luna.

"Thank you."

Ephraim began to calm inwardly—Luna's attention and nearness soothed him. She wasn't afraid to look at him. He sought to glance at her whenever possible. Her eyes were alive and sparkling! She seemed very interested in him! She talked with him—face-to-face! Perhaps things would turn out for the best this time.

ↀↀↀ

The official season of killing began early in the morning. Two camouflaged bow hunters entered Designated Area 2 from the parking lot in High Point State Park. Almost four thousand park acres had been defined for deer harvesting. They headed to the specific lowland location they had scouted in the summer.

If they had walked farther that summer, they would have discovered a gray mansion at the end of the hunting region.

"Sure you have your refuge permit with you, Ken?"

"Yeah. Remember to turn your cell phone to vibrate to tell me of a kill."

"Done already."

"Me too."

The two stepped out of the car to the quiet of a mild, calm autumn awakening. Skeleton trees, naked bushes, and brown landscape surrounded them. They took slow careful steps after entering the woods. Walking on the brittle dry leaves could be noisy.

The bow hunters placed toe first then weight on the heel, so they wouldn't announce themselves to their game, always aware of any black bears forging for a last meal before winter sleep.

Ken licked his index finger then held it up to check the wind—it was in his face so human smell wouldn't precede them but, as a precaution, they both had rubbed on deer musk.

It took an hour at this pace to reach their destination.

"There—" Ken pointed to a platform high up in an oak tree. "—that's mine."

"I'm off to the right. Good luck!"

"You too, Russ."

Russ quietly pushed his way through thickets and

saplings. He was looking up to find his stand when he tripped.

"Damn it!" Getting up, Russ turned around to see what he had stumbled over. "Jesus Christ! Ken! Ken, get over here!" Russ called, breaking the morning silence.

"Quiet, man. What's up?"

"Get over here! Look at this. Look at this!"

"What? I'm half way up the tree!"

"Get your ass over here!"

Ken trotted over. "What is it?"

"I tripped over a part of—this! Come here!"

A skinned half-eaten carcass lay at their feet. Sinews had been torn off exposing white bone. Graying flesh had been stripped and flowed like ribbons on the forest floor. Large chunks of muscle were missing.

"Is that a bear? Christ, what happened to it?"

"I don't know? What could have brought down a bear? Do bears eat other bears?

"Bears don't skin prey. Where are the paws?"

"Wait a minute, wait a minute! Look at the head. There's no snout and the teeth, the teeth definitely seem human."

"Oh." Russ turned away as recognition hit him in the stomach. "Christ, it is!"

"Crap! Call nine-one-one!"

An hour later, Davy, Soldering, Jay, Brenson, and paramedics trampled through the woods, broadcasting their arrival before they could be seen.

"What the hell would a body be doing way out here?" Soldering asked no one in particular.

"I think this is one of our missing initial couple," Jay proposed.

"What makes you say that?"

"Well, Lieutenant, Robinson was found far from here, and I assume Brenda Armstead would be nearby the murder scene if she hasn't run off. Since we haven't found either Vincent Marconi or Dawn Portny, this could be one of them."

They spotted the rattled hunters sitting near a tree. As the group approached, Ken pointed to an area far from the tree. Davy cautiously edged nearer and studied the carcass. "No hands or feet. Teeth are intact. It's a good thing you obtained DNA samples as well, Sergeant, since we don't have complete dental records for Marconi or Portny. We'll soon know. We need to remove this as quickly as possible. And at this time, we don't need to inform the mayor till we know more.

Dr. Brenson moved forward and examined the remains. "It definitely is human. Not much more I can tell now."

"Time and cause of death Doctor?"

"Putrefaction has begun. Probably bloating, but the tears and rips have caused the release of gas and fluids. So maybe three to four days, maybe more. I can't determine the cause of death because of the condition, Lieutenant. No signs of fractures except for bite marks on bone—at this moment, I would say a bear has been fat-tening up on this food source. The skinning and exposure will also cause some problems. This flaying seems surgi-cal so while a bear may have eaten parts, I don't think it's a bear kill. But who could have done this?"

"Bears are denning this time of year, so the feed makes sense, but where did it get it?" Soldering won-dered aloud.

"If it is a bear, the den might be nearby, so we better hurry."

"Right, we have to act immediately on this, no time to gather a search party. You and I and the lieutenant will look for drag marks that may lead us to the killing spot after we search the immediate area. Dr. Brenson will re-turn with the body."

ᏋᏇᏇ

"Is anyone aware that you are here, Ash?"

"Why do you ask?"

"I do not want anyone else coming here."

"Don't worry, Ephraim, I haven't told anyone. Your privacy is safe."

"Good, good, this is very good."

"Listen, I want to tell you about Wicca."

"Wicca?"

"Yes. It's a belief in the goodness of nature and en-joyment of life."

"It is a religion?"

"I guess you could call it that."

"Is this like the Church of England?"

"I don't know about the Church of England. Wicca has many deities both male and female that guide us through life, that allow us to be who we are and what we will be."

"I do not understand."

"Let me get my altar set in the car and we can form a circle. I think you'll understand then."

"Ash!" Luna reached her hand out to call him back, but he had left again to get his athame, bowls, chalk, and notes. She sat with her legs crossed, arms folded in her lap, glancing down and waiting for his return. Without Ash, she felt uncomfortable. The silence was strong and she felt Ephraim inching his way toward her.

"Do you like music?" she almost shouted to break the awful silence and divert Ephraim.

It worked. Ephraim stopped.

"Certainly. My uncle has a magnificent record collection."

"Your Uncle? Is he here now?"

"Unfortunately, he passed several years back. But I feel he is near when I listen to the Victrola. Music helps me to endure and I find comfort within it."

Music has charms to soothe the savage beast, Luna thought.

"Do you like music?" he asked.

"Yes."

"Perhaps we could listen together. The collection is vast and includes classical and modern like Sinatra and Brightman."

Luna stared at the door, willing Ash to return. "That would be nice."

Ash retrieved the bundle from the back seat. He had been waiting a long time for this—his own coven. Everything had to go right. He practiced in a low whisper, "Eko, Eko, Azarak."

It couldn't sound rote or too dramatic. He had to be perfect to impress. This would be the best day of his life!

Ephraim stared at Luna's partially exposed thighs— soft white skin leading to pleasure. She was enticing. He was sure she wanted him now with this brazen exposure. His excitement grew.

They had so much in common and Angelina had never been this friendly and alluring. His emotions welled and took control. "Angelina!"

Luna looked up, expecting to see someone else in the kitchen.

"Angelina, I am so glad you have once again come back." Ephraim walked to the kitchen door and locked it. He faced Luna, rubbing his crotch with his left hand. "We have been through so much, and now I truly know you want me! I cannot wait."

"What? What are you doing? What do you mean?"

"I have missed you, my love."

"My—what? Stay away. W—what are you doing?" Luna stammered again and started to get up.

"Please do not act this way. Do not tease me. I know you desire me too, I know this."

"You have it wrong. You misunderstood something."

"No, no, my love. I have not." Ephraim advanced with a gleam in his eyes and a grotesque smile on his face. He unbuttoned his trousers.

"Ash! Ash!" Luna yelled as she hastily backed across the kitchen, startled and frightened at his actions.

Ephraim unveiled his erection as a gift to her.

"Oh my God! Stay away from me! Go away! Ash! Ash!"

Ephraim continued his steady advance.

Luna screamed at the horror approaching.

Ephraim placed his right hand on her mouth, alarmed over her suddenly changed attitude. "No, not again! You like me. I saw that! You like me!"

Luna desperately struggled to get away. Ephraim pushed her to the floor and positioned his hands around her neck. "Please stop! I do not want to do this again."

Luna tried to pull his grip off her throat. She kicked, squirmed, and rolled. Nothing worked. Ephraim had been through this before.

Ephraim moved on top of her. "If it must be this way again, so be it."

The door knob rattled.

"What's going on? Luna, did you scream? Luna!"

Ash tried the door again. "Open this door! Why is it locked? Let me in!"

Ephraim positioned his right hand on her throat and started to open her blouse with the other.

Luna's scream was muffled by his huge hand. She tasted acid and metal. Ephraim's large head was above her. She smelled something fishy. She felt his rough hand on her breast.

The lack of air tricked her mind into believing this was a dream—she started to faint, to retreat from this repulsive violation, but she came back to reality at the sound of glass fracturing.

Ash had thrown the altar bundle through the kitchen window and climbed in. It took long seconds for Ash to register the scene before him. "What the fuck are you doing?"

"You have brought back Angelina, Ash."

"Who? What? Get off her, you creep!"

Ephraim stared at Ash. He knew this would come and he was sad, but Angelina meant more than friendship. He rolled off Luna, quickly went to a kitchen drawer, and removed a meat tenderizer.

Hopping on a chair, then onto the table, he jumped at Ash. "I am sorry this time, Ash!"

Ash moved aside, pushing Ephraim in midair. He landed against the refrigerator and slid down, slightly dazed. Ash retrieved his altar bundle, removed the athame, and pointed it toward the slumped figure.

Without turning his head, he called behind him, "Luna, Luna, are you all right?"

Luna sat up rubbing her throat. She was too shocked to realize exactly what had just happened, too stunned to speak.

"Luna, come with me." Eying Ephraim, Ash reached behind him and found Luna's arm. Pulling her up, he advanced toward the door, keeping the knife in the direction of a dejected, silent Ephraim.

Ash helped Luna into the car, all the while repeating, "I'm sorry, I'm so sorry." He sped away without looking back.

ↃↄↃↄ

The three men followed a path of disturbed leaves and broken brush to the border of the swamp. The partially submerged red car was easy to spot. Nothing could be seen inside through the dried muck and branches covering it.

The lieutenant quickly called Harper's Towing.

Jay walked a faint trail to Hankins Road to await Harper. With the help of Randy Mcgreen, Bill maneuvered his tow truck to the swamp's edge.

"Christ! This looks like Vince's ride, Bill!"

"Well, we'll soon see, Randy. Let's get it out."

Mcgreen waded in and attached a steel cable to the bumper mounting point of the submerged car.

The black ooze initially refused to give up its catch.

Bill pulled for thirty seconds then rested the power winch. Another pull lifted the back end and slid it onto firm ground.

Davy opened the sludge-coated driver's door. Fetid slimy water, three mud minnows, and clumps of rot rushed out. A soggy lump was in the cab. Soaked shoes and dark stained clothes barely identified it as human. "From the size, this looks male and the position is just as we found Robinson. And the car was underwater. I don't believe in coincidences. Bill, take the car with the body directly to the St Claire's—I don't want to wait for the doctor to return here. Lieutenant and Sergeant, we'll search the immediate vicinity for anything else before we move forward. I'm willing to bet the body we found back there was Dawn Portny."

It was early afternoon that the hungry and tired trio heard music before noticing smoke ahead lazily swirling up masking the somber sky. Yellow and orange filtered through the trees as they neared. Cackling sounds and waves of heat made it apparent that something was on fire.

Music drifted with the heat. It became louder and clearer as they neared a burning structure. The harsh forceful whispers of the flames and the collapsing of walls couldn't muffle the sound. It persisted from the center of the manor, despite its hellish surroundings.

"Someone is still in there!"

"If so, there's no helping now, Sergeant."

The men stood fascinated, listening and watching the large gray manor consume itself.

"What is that music?" Jay asked, caught up in the melody.

"It sounds like, 'Time to Say Goodbye,'" Davy answered, "by Andrea Bocelli and Sarah Brightman. My wife is a fan of Brightman."

"It's beautiful!"

"Yes, part is in Italian."

Mesmerized by flame and music, no one immediately thought to call the fire department. Each knew that by the time the engines would arrive, the fire would be tame. Fire and song hypnotized them into immobility. When the main floor collapsed into the cellar, the music ended. The flames hid in embers. The manor became a pile of black bones and released memories in light smoke. Soldering called it in. Without the blaze and music to attract them, the men returned to the reality of the search and began to look around. Soldering and Jay entered the vacant barn, picking up a discarded bucket. Davy noticed a recently disturbed patch of ground near what appeared to be a small cemetery.

EPILOGUE

Though all the missing couples were found, the reasons for their deaths were not. Mayor Zicker issued a statement that drugged-crazed itinerants had inhabited the now burnt house and were most likely responsible for the deaths. The recorded owner had been listed as deceased many years ago, even though taxes and utilities were still automatically paid. The Healthy Place food store delivered groceries, but never saw anyone. These facts were withheld.

A state wide alert was routinely posted for any itinerants, but without descriptions of any kind, little was expected. The mayor was happy to report these unknown killers had left Hamburg and announced the case closed. He resumed normal village governing.

After a painful week of funeral services—four closed caskets and one open—Paul rested beside his daughter. The community was happy to be relieved of its worry and rapidly regarded these incidents as merely aberrations. All looked forward to Thanksgiving, except for those immediately affected who quietly slipped from the Hamburg conscious. Life resumed, as ignorant as before.

Special Agent James Davy did not officially close the cases and the folders remained on his desk.

New Jersey State Troopers returned to their long list of crimes.

The Hamburg Police Department filed the cases and returned to investigating snow plows damaging mailboxes and violations of winter parking regulations. In a show of completion and government and law enforcement competency, Lieutenant Soldering was advanced to chief and Sergeant Hurray made lieutenant. Jay had his excitement and was content that the return to mundane allowed him to be with his family.

Dr. Brenson was promoted to chief of emergency medicine and moved into a gray colonial that came on the market located on Bluffs Court.

After several days of mutual silence, Ash and Luna reunited. Both agreed not to talk about what had happened and chose to believe that vagrants were ultimately responsible for the deaths. They went to the junior prom and, despite expectations, had an enjoyable time. Both remained Goths, but Ash gave up Wicca and, upon Luna's insistence, started to attend Lutheran masses.

Superintendent Bonner left for another school district, haunted by what he had seen that one night in the parking lot and what someone now knew.

After a few weeks of interest, the Gingerbread Castle and mill were forgotten again and continued to decay. Each day brought less hope of a revival.

Somewhere in Pennsylvania, a sleek Firemist Charcoal four-door Buick Regal sedan with black tinted windows glided at night through small towns, looking for occupied parked cars.

About the Author

R. James Milos graduated from Seton Hall University with a BS in Education. Milos joined the Peace Corps as a teacher of English as a foreign language (TEFL) serving two years in Baghlan, Afghanistan. Now living in Southwick, Massachusetts, his career has included teaching English in New Jersey and professional positions in communication and documentation. He has published three books: *The Kush*, *The Troop,* and a novella: *Miles from Millersburg.*

He is married with two adult children, Stephanie and Greg, and three grandchildren, Travis, Daphne, and Vivian.

"All living things communicate—some better than others."